CONFE

is

Good for the Soul

CONFESSION
is
Good for the Soul

A Clive Thompson Investigates Novel III

SUSAN WILLIS

Also By Susan Willis

Intriguing Journeys at Christmas
Joseph is Missing
Death at the Caravan Park
The Curious Casefiles
Magazine Stories from the North East
Christmas Shambles in York
Clive's Christmas Crusades
The Christmas Tasters
The Guest for Christmas Lunch
The Man Who Loved Women
Dark Room Secrets
His Wife's Secret
The Bartlett Family Secrets
Northern Bake Off
You've Got Cake
A Business Affair
Is He Having an Affair
NO, CHEF, I Won't!

Prologue

He'd remembered the sight and sounds of the flames along with the acrid taste of smoke in the back of his throat, and later the smell of smouldering ash. He'd loved the flames in the fire. The colours and height. The strength and force. The howling noise.

Chapter One

I'm standing on Market Street near The Jorvik Centre in York, and don't mind admitting I am a tad nervous. I've walked down from home for an interview at a PI agency, and my palms are sweating. I rub them down my new chinos. The collar of the blue dress shirt I'm wearing is irritating my neck, and I bristle while running my fingers along the edge - it's years since I've done anything like this.

Standing outside a newish block of office spaces, I know these must be expensive to rent and can't help wondering how the owner, Geoff, can afford this. Maybe there's more money in private investigations than I realise.

Geoff had told me on the phone that he was inundated with requests for help and needed an assistant. 'I've heard about your success solving the suspicious death at Whitley Bay caravan park, Clive,' he'd said. 'And with your knowledge of the city on historic tours and, your previous crusades with muggings, pickpockets, and neighbourhood burglaries it'll stand you in good stead.'

I'd felt my cheeks flush, never knowing how to handle compliments. I was flattered, of course, but wary - I've always thought I didn't want to be a PI.

I take a deep breath and remember my fiancé, Barbara's words of encouragement at breakfast. 'Just go along and get the feel of it, Clive. If it's not for you, then you don't have to take it.'

I inhale another big breath and let it out slowly, then press the intercom button on the modern office block. I'm buzzed-in and begin to climb a flight of stairs. There's a strong smell of freshly laid marble-grey carpet and raw wood. I look down at the skirting boards which haven't been painted as yet. The stark newness seems creepy, and when I hear a low whirling noise, I feel a shiver run up my back.

I expect the banging pipe noises and creaking sounds in an old property like our house, but not in a new build. I look up ahead as I mount the stairs, and with slightly trembling knees, I reach the top. I'm standing in front of two white doors with a photocopying machine in between them spewing out realms of paper. Phew, I think, that's what the whirling noise is and shake away my silly notions.

The first white door has a bronze plaque with "Geoff Smithson, PI" inscribed on it, and I trace my finger along the gold lettering, nodding in admiration. Somehow, I'd had a different impression in my mind after watching the TV show, "Strike," which is based in a rundown area of London. Cormoran Strike, played by Tom Burke, is a retired soldier who solves grisly murders. Not that we have such crimes here in York, well, not yet anyway, but Strike's office is small and shabby.

Geoff's office appears to be the exact opposite as I open the door and step inside. The room looks like a trendy, spacious office with two desks. Dark grey carpet covers the floor, the walls are white, with two long windows and light grey blinds shielding the direct sunlight. One wall has a huge shelving unit and three big filing cabinets.

A tall man jumps up from his desk and hurries around to greet me. The first thought I have is that his grey suit and white shirt blend into the room's décor. He's taller than me and slim with a good firm handshake.

Geoff says, 'Have a seat, Clive.'

I perch on the edge of the chair in front of his desk. Settled opposite me in his big white swivel chair, I can tell he is sizing me up, as I am him. Thank God, I followed Barbara's advice and ditched my jeans and T-Shirt. This guy has style, I think admiring his blue Italian leather loafers which he is wearing without socks. I often wonder about this and whether your feet get sore without the comfortable layer of a good pair of socks. I shake the stupid thoughts from my head and try to concentrate.

'So pleased you could come along today,' he says. 'I'm out of the office for the rest of this week.'

He gives me a friendly, warm smile and I return the gesture.

'That's okay,' I say. 'Thanks for taking the time out to see me.'

I lick my dry lips, hoping this is a polite response to his comment. I'd read an article on Google and brushed up on interview etiquette so I wouldn't make a fool of myself. This appeared to be a good answer because Geoff nods and smiles again offering me a coffee. His smile is tight-lipped, and I decide it's a shame about his crooked stained teeth which spoil his natural good looks.

I thank Geoff and watch him walk over to the empty desk where there's a coffee percolator brewing. I figure, with a smattering of grey in his thick black hair and sideburns he's in his early forties but obviously has a much younger outlook on life.

Accepting milk but refusing sugar, I relax my shoulders.

'I'm not looking upon this an interview, as such, Clive,' he says. 'More of an informal get together and chat.'

I smile and sit further back in my chair while he places the coffee mug in front of me. I know the role of a private investigator involves taking pictures, gathering information, and compiling evidence for court cases, interviewing witnesses, and doing research. All of this I'd be comfortable with and know I can do well, and without hesitation. But I wonder if the role entails more than Geoff had told me on the phone call.

Our introduction had come from a friend of a colleague in the travel agency, and we discuss this. 'Yeah,' I say. 'York is a big city but in some respects it's a small community too.'

Geoff nods, 'Well, I was mighty impressed when I heard about the death at Whitley Bay last year and how you'd solved the case,' he says.

I've just taken a gulp of coffee and feel my cheeks flush. Whether it's with embarrassment or warmth from the mug, I don't know, but say, 'Oh, I wouldn't call it a case, more of helping out the caravan park owner because she was alone with a missing elderly mother.'

Geoff winks. 'Oh, we can never resist a damsel in distress, can we?'

I'm not sure how to take this but remembering Liz, with her low-cut tops, colourful language, and flock of pink hair, I smile. 'Well, I wouldn't put it quite like that.'

His grey eyes glint. 'Ah, pull the other on, it's got bells on!'

I'm wondering how he's got this impression about me and know I need to put him right straight away. 'It was purely on a friendship basis, Geoff, because I have my amazing fiancé, Barbara who is one in a million.'

I see him shuffle around on his swivel chair and he mutters, 'Yes, yes, of course.'

He takes a gulp of his coffee and I wonder if he's a Jack-the-lad who plays around with other women? The sun peeps through a gap in the blind and glistens off his gold wedding ring. I presume he's married but of course this doesn't mean to say it's a happy marriage. I'm hoping I haven't unnerved him with my answer and give him a big friendly smile. I ask, 'So, can you tell me exactly what work I would be involved with?'

Geoff makes a steeple with his fingers and leans forward over his desk. He lowers his voice and says, 'Okay, but this is strictly confidential as I'm sure you'll appreciate. The casefiles and different investigations on the shelves need to be typed-up from my notebook scribblings and then filed. The oldest one is a deathbed confession from a sergeant in the army who confessed to his son that he'd shot a man in the war for being a coward.'

Instantly, my antennae are on red alert. I want to shout, wow, that's an amazing story, but don't. I take a deep breath and nod sincerely.

Geoff continues, 'Then once I've done my enquiries if I think there's a crime to investigate further, I refer it to the police,' he says. 'In the future, you could get involved with other enquiries that's if you want to, of course, however, for now it's more general research, recording and filing.'

I smile thinking of the secrecy and how Geoff would fit well into MI 5.

'So,' I ask. 'It's a bit of a secretarial post?'

He shakes his head. 'It may seem like that at first, but I want someone with an insight into difficult situations who can think ahead and solve problems by talking to people. And yes, if I'm out on secondments then you'll need to answer the phone, make appointments and generally run the office, but from what I've heard, and now upon meeting you, I can tell you're a people's person.'

I pull back my shoulders wondering if his choice of word, secondment means following people? I'd already decided I wouldn't be comfortable doing this as it can be an invasion of a person's privacy. However, I must admit last year when I'd followed the German caravaner and discovered he was the main suspect, I'd been very excited and justified in my suspicions. Also, with being an author, I class myself as a good judge of character and it had been a powerful test of my observational skills.

Geoff continues, 'Can I ask why you use your second name because on your CV it states, Gordon Clive Thompson?'

'Ah, well,' I say and sigh. 'I've never liked either name to be honest but figured years ago that I dislike Gordon more. And when I started writing, I figured, Clive Thompson had a nice old-fashioned ring to it, especially when I saw it in print on the front of my paperback novel.'

I have a flashback to schooldays when I hated the name Gordon. I can still hear the kids shout, Gordon-the-Gopher. At the time, I'd asked Mum why they choose the two names, but she'd been too drunk to remember. Dad hadn't been much help either because he had been stoned.

Geoff nods. 'Okay, so the assistant's job will be two days a week. 9-5pm. At first, it'll be to clear my back-log at an hourly rate of £14 and expenses for travelling etc. Then after a month we could reassess - that's if you'd like to join me?'

I sit further back in the chair and ponder. It would fit in with my part-time travel agency job, and the generous salary will help towards paying for our wedding. Self-publishing my two books on Amazon means they are selling quite well, but I don't think I'll ever make six figures in royalties. However, this amount, along with travel agency wages, and tips I make from the York tours, all adds to the monthly coffers.

Barbara, bless her, keeps telling me it doesn't matter, and she can keep us afloat financially and give us a good wedding day. But I don't want that. I look down at my hands clasped together. She paid for our first Christmas together when I'd been furloughed so it doesn't seem fair to take money from her savings now. Plus, I would like to think that in two years I had made some progress and was in a better place financially. I brighten knowing after a month that I can decide to continue or not.

'This sounds right up my street,' I say, knowing I'd be a fool to refuse.

Getting up from the chair, I hold out my hand and Geoff shakes it firmly.

'That's great news, Clive,' he says. 'Welcome on board – I'm sure we'll get along well together.'

I turn to leave and walk towards the door when Geoff calls, 'Oh, Clive. I don't suppose you can start tomorrow?'

I chortle and agree. Hoping upon hope I've made the right decision I run down the stairs and out into the sunshine.

Chapter Two

I pull our front door shut behind me on Victor Street and head off towards my first day at work. Barbara, who I always call Barbie, went down to Manchester last night to start a three day food-styling project with a photographer. For over ten years now she's been self-employed and works for different food suppliers anywhere in the UK.

She knows I'm feeling a mixture of trepidation and excitement for this new job. Last night, I'd told her, 'I just feel totally out of my comfort zone.'

After our three years together, Barbie knows me inside and out. I never hide anything from her after my disastrous start when we first met. I hadn't told her about my past because I'd been too embarrassed. But when it all eventually came out, she'd forgiven my transgression and given us a second chance. Thank God, she believed in us, or shall I say, in me. She has my heart and soul, a little poetic for me, but it's how I feel.

She'd sent a reassuring text this morning from the Manchester hotel. 'Have a great day, darling – you've got this!'

I'd grinned, wolfed down breakfast and drank two mugs of strong coffee.

***

I head down to the office through Coppergate, the open-air shopping centre and stop to smile at the alleyway with symmetrical rows of multi-coloured umbrellas suspended from wires. It's a chic area of the city and a few shoppers are out already.

Geoff is in the office when I arrive, and he gives me a spare key. He's dressed in casual jeans and a sweatshirt although I can tell they look designer, good quality jeans.

He explains, 'I was suited and booted yesterday because I'd been to see a client, but ordinarily we only need to be smart in the office if we have meetings or a consultation.'

I nod and smile deciding I'll follow his example tomorrow. We have coffee together before he leaves for an assignment in Glasgow. When he hands me a mug and I sit at my desk, I smell a waft of cigarette smoke hanging around him. Ah, I think, that's the reason for his stained teeth – he's a smoker.

I unpack a small bag in which I've brought pens, my diary, and other desk paraphernalia. Geoff walks around the office, and I follow him. He apologises and shows me his haphazard filing system in the cabinet. I sigh knowing this will be the first thing to re-organise because I can't work in chaos.

He lifts out a slim brown folder from the cabinet and plonks it on my desk. 'This is the case I mentioned yesterday about the soldier's deathbed confession,' he says. 'So, can you start with that first because it's the oldest.'

I nod. 'Yeah, I'm looking forward to reading about it all.'

Geoff points to the door and says, 'Oh, and the toilets are downstairs on the ground floor – we share with the other offices.'

I nod and spot a small fridge in the corner. Last night Barbie had made me a lunch container and I pop it in the fridge while explaining how she is a food technologist.

I say, 'Barbie hates the amount of junk food I eat when she's not around.'

Geoff grins. 'Ahh, I can see now that she is one in a million!'

We smile and I enjoy the relaxed atmosphere which feels much easier than yesterday. While I'm arranging things on my desk, I learn how Geoff lives on Tower Street. This leads onto Friar Street, an old, but upmarket area in York across from the famous Cliff Tower. These properties are Edwardian and over Skeldergate Bridge from where our small, but perfectly formed, two-bed terraced house is situated.

'Hey,' I say. 'We're just about neighbours – well, there's only the river between us.'

Geoff laughs. 'Yeah, that's true. But our house belongs to my wife, Margaret who lived there with her parents long before I met her,' he says. 'She's an interior designer and if I say so myself, is brilliant at what she does.'

Jeez, I bet she charges a pretty packet for her services, I think, but say, 'So, we both have strong business women behind us.'

Geoff pulls a comical face. 'And don't we know it!'

I chortle and sip my coffee. Geoff asks about my books, and I launch into my usual pitch of how I started writing. 'Well, aged eighteen, I worked as a labourer and studied at night to gain my English A level then did a writing course. I began as many others have done by writing short stories and progressed to my first novel. But as a debut author, I struggled to find a publisher and rather than have the book doing nothing I learnt how to publish it on Amazon,' I say and smile. 'This first novel is set in

London because many crime books are for some reason, but my second is a story based in Durham.'

Geoff's face looks animated. 'Hey, that's great – I love reading crime novels and thrillers,' he says grabbing his iPad. 'I'm downloading them both now so I can read them tonight when I'm doing surveillance.'

This makes me wonder how he can take his eye off the suspect to read, but figure, unlike me, he's probably very experienced and can do both things at once. I'm delighted at his gesture and thank him profusely as I do with anyone who wants to read my work.

Geoff begins to pack up his mobile, iPad, and laptop into a brown soft-leather holdall which I can tell must have cost at least £500 if not more. I admit to feeling slightly envious.

He grimaces and says, 'Well, I'm in awe of anyone who can put that number of words down on paper – as you'll see from my notes, I struggle writing records - it was one of the reasons I left the force.'

With that, and before I get the chance to ask more, he claps me on the shoulder and hurries past saying, 'Just ring if you need to find anything.'

At the close of the door, I push my chair back and smile knowing I'm going to enjoy this job and new challenge. I think again of the TV programme, "Strike" and his new assistant, Holiday Grainger who played the part. I remember how she started as a newbie in Cormoran's office and tackled the job.

I get cracking sorting out everything from the shelves into organised piles with an alphabet index system. The morning flies over and by the time I open my lunch box I feel upbeat at what I've achieved in the space of a few hours. The sandwich is my favourite tuna and mayonnaise. Happily, I tuck-in while opening the brown folder and begin to read.

The very words, deathbed confession makes my head spin with ideas for different stories or the inclusion in a novel. What state of mind must someone be in to confess a major transgression like this, I wonder?

I Google the words deathbed confessions and read many posts. The first states, this is an admittance from someone who is nearing or on their deathbed. The confession may help alleviate any guilt, regrets, or sins that the dying person may have had in their life. The person may want to live the last moments free of secrets they could have been holding their entire life. The confession can be given to anyone, but it's usually to a family member or loved one. Doctors and nurses often hear a deathbed confession because they are present in a person's last moments.

On the first page, Geoff has written, William Riley 1939 – 2022 RIP.

Ooh, nice start, I think and discover, Sergeant William Riley had died when he was ninety years old. He'd confessed to his seventy year old son, Jack that he'd shot a man called Private Jones because he was a coward and had tried to run away from the fighting. They'd both been in the Durham Light Infantry and had been miners at the same colliery.

I sit back again deep in thought and sip a carton of juice. I try to imagine the scene with Jack sitting at his father's deathbed and how he'd felt when this bombshell had been dropped. If, of course, he'd been a loving devoted father to his son and a decent man then a major confession like this would have been devastating.

Jack had told Geoff how his father had been a pillar of the community and hard-working all his life. He'd stayed in the army until retirement and his wife died of a stroke in her early eighties. They'd only ever had Jack and hadn't wanted more children. 'More to the point,' Jack had said, 'Sergeant Riley hadn't been home much to make any more babies.'

Jack had grown up spoilt by his mother and had disappointed his father by not joining the army. In the argument which ensued, Jack had recited a phrase he'd heard and told his father, 'You can't live off your parents success – you have to live your own life and gain your own achievements.'

Jack stated adamantly that he wasn't going down the mines either, being slightly claustrophobic and joined the East Coast Railway in his twenties. However, when Sergeant Riley boarded the first train Jack drove, his chest had swelled with pride, although he never told his son this – it didn't do to praise kids too much.

In his later days in the nursing home, Sergeant Riley had been one of their most popular residents. He'd been friendly, with an optimistic outlook and joked with all the carers – they'd all loved him.

This is good to hear, I think because if he'd been a low-life waste of space like my own father, then this crime wouldn't have been so shocking. I shudder. In fact, if I'd been given news like this, I wouldn't have been the slightest bit surprised that my father was capable of such an act. He'd been a drug addict and during most of my childhood, he had been so far out of it, he wouldn't have noticed if I was present in the house or not.

I'd had, as Barbie often says, a troubled upbringing. Aged fourteen I'd nicked stuff to buy booze. At first it had been for my alcoholic mother and then I got to like the effect when I drank. The alcohol took me away from all the crap in the house and it also impressed my mates. I had got mixed up with a bad crowd although at the time I'd been pleased to be accepted into their gang. It was better than fending for myself and at least they'd wanted to spend time with me - which had been more than my parents did.

However, I'd ignored warning after warning from social workers until I had ended up in a young offenders' institution aged fifteen. I spent three years there and was released on my eighteenth birthday. One of the team leaders had called it a short sharp shock and it worked.

Never again have I drunk more than a single glass of wine or beer, and although I wouldn't admit this to other men because it's not macho, I don't particularly like the taste anymore. And I might add here, since then, I've never taken a thing that didn't belong to me and wasn't mine.

I shrug the memories aside and begin to type Geoff's document. It's true that his writing is as bad as a doctors scrawl on a prescription pad, but I persevere trying to decipher words as I type. Geoff's case notes, however, are fascinating. I re-edit his sentences depicting the events into a more legible order of how things happened when he met Jack.

I'm so engrossed that when the landline on Geoff's desk begins to ring, I'm startled. I pick up and answer politely, 'Hello, Geoff Smithson PI agency. How can I help you?'

A female voice says, 'Ah, sorry, I must have misdialled. I was hoping to speak to Geoff?'

I realise she doesn't know who I am and introduce myself then ask, 'Have you tried his mobile?'

'Yeah, but it's switched off, I think,' she says, with an impatient edge to her voice. 'But when you do speak to him can you tell him, Jemma rang, and it's urgent that he calls me back!'

I agree and she hangs up.

And, there's another mystery to mull over, I think and smile. I know his wife is called Margaret, but my voice of reason kicks in - she could, of course, be a client. However, when I'd listened to Jemma, I'm sure I detected a Scottish accent. And Geoff is now driving up to Glasgow.

Hmm, just a coincidence, I think rubbing my chin. I try not to put two and two together and give Geoff the benefit of the doubt but maybe my first impression of him yesterday was correct. And, as Barbie's Mam would say, perhaps he has a hungry eye for the ladies.

Chapter Three

The following morning I'm back in the office, and as they say, bright-eyed and bushy-tailed. I'd not had time to finish typing up Geoff's notes and know it's my first task for the day. Geoff had rang before I left yesterday. I'd given him the message from Jemma and told him about re-organising the filing system. He hadn't commented about the call but had been delighted about the re-organisation.

All is well, I think re-opening the document at the place where I'd finished. I decide to make a separate set of my own notes because the case is intriguing. I want to write my thoughts as I read what happened.

Geoff's record tells me how he'd gone to visit seventy-year old, Jack, to see exactly what he could do to help after his father's confession. Jack didn't have a computer and wasn't online, therefore, he didn't know where to start contacting the army and tracing people on social media.

I'd wondered how Geoff had got involved in this as a PI and now I know. It's strange to think there are people who aren't active online nowadays but there are, especially the elderly and people with disabilities. At the grand old age of thirty two, I'm too young to remember much of a life without the internet and social media but the elderly can and I feel sorry for them.

It's as though they're being left behind as many daily activities now are conducted online with the demise of the high street. We have an elderly neighbour who has changed her bank account because the local branch has closed.

She'd looked at me dumbstruck during the pandemic when I mentioned grocery home deliveries and Barbie had done her shopping when she was sheltered because of her age. We'd carry her shopping each week, leave it on the doorstep, ring her doorbell, then stand well back on the path while she opened her door.

I'd often sit on the wall after cutting the grass and chat to her because her family couldn't travel up from Leeds, so she saw no one other than us on a daily basis. She'd sit on a stool in her doorway and tell me all about York. Not the old history because I know that with doing historical tours, but how the city was in the fifties and sixties.

I sigh now, there were many people, especially the vulnerable elderly who'd suffered during the pandemic. But, I cheered, at least she was protected and didn't get the dreaded Covid virus.

I think of Barbie now because she is from Co-Durham in a small town called Chester-le Street. This is where her mam still lives aged, eighty-seven. I always call her Mrs Webster although she's told me repeatedly to use her first name, Connie, but I can't - it's simply a mark of respect. She's an amazing woman for her age and I could listen to her forever when she talks about the past especially her travels on holidays. She's a true socialist through and through. I ring her to ask about the Durham Light Infantry knowing their office is at Elvet Waterside in the city.

Mrs Webster tells me about the significance of the DLI in the area. During the First World War 1000s of volunteers from the mines, shipyards, farms, shops, schools, offices and industries of County Durham joined the DLI. They fought in every major battle of the Great War. And, during the Second World War, nine battalions fought with distinction from Dunkirk up to D-Day to the final defeat of Nazi Germany in 1945.

I look back to Geoff's notes where the correspondence had been via email, and he'd printed out their response. By using old documents, the DLI helped Geoff to trace the family of Private Jones who had been shot. In The Great War many soldiers were executed for cowardice but there were no charges to be brought against Sergent Riley. They would simply record the incident.

I can't begin to imagine how a young guy would feel fighting in France, and being terrified in the knowledge he was probably going to be killed. In fact, I can't imagine what army life would feel like per se. I wouldn't like the discipline, the orders, the marching, and the uniforms where I'd look the same as hundreds of other men. I would hate the loss of my own identity as me, Clive Thompson, a one-off in every sense of the word. Of course, there was the common cause to fight for King and country and win freedom from the Germans, but I'm not a brave, heroic type of guy. In fact, I think I might have been tempted to run away with Private Jones.

Barbie's father had been a miner and I remember how we'd taken Mrs Webster to visit Redhills last year. The bright red sign had said, Durham Miners' Hall – The Home of the Pitman's Parliament. On that day, she'd told us about the annual Durham Miners' Gala in July and how it had always been a great day out where miners marched with their colliery banners and their own brass bands.

Apparently, this year there'd been 300,000 people crammed into the quaint narrow streets of the small city. It was a celebration of North East Trade Unions with good speeches and an amazing atmosphere. Following the pandemic, key workers were celebrated because there'd been very little gratitude shown by the government in their pay packets for the many lives they'd saved.

This makes me wonder about the latest train strikes and if trade unions are making a big come-back? I'm not political at all but I do know we have to move forwards and going backwards with anything in life doesn't work. In my humble opinion striking only affects the general public who deserve a service and better customer relations. It's best to talk through grievances and negotiate pay deals rather than walk away empty handed in a huff. And yes, disruption causes companies to lose money, but this means they'll have even less profits to award pay deals in the future.

Geoff has written how he'd gone back to Jack's home in Durham with his findings. He had helped Jack write a letter of apology to Private Jones family who now live in Newcastle. However, when Geoff had gone, Jack had stared at the letter and thought it through deciding this may give the family even more grief.

There were two reasons why he hadn't licked the stamp that day. First, would finding out that Private Jones had been a coward be more upsetting? And second, being shot by a sergeant in his own infantry could be equally, if not more, upsetting. Jack had thought of his father's saying and decided to let sleeping dogs lie.

Whilst there, Geoff had been offered tea in the lounge while Jack's wife, Sheila lay upstairs in bed. She had breast cancer with a poor prognosis and was recovering from her last chemotherapy.

God, I think, this poor bloke had been through a hard time. Not only had he just lost his father, but it looked as though his wife wouldn't be with him for much longer either. Further notes tell me that Jack was a retired train driver. He worked all his life for LNER and loved York Railway Museum, although he hadn't visited for a good many years. Geoff wrote that he wasn't a good-looking man but mentioned a certain charm and genial personality.

I grin reading the next sentence. When he was younger, Jack admitted to having girlfriends in some of the major train stations, Peterborough, Edinburgh and of course, London King's Cross.

I think about Geoff, which of course I don't know for sure, and now Jack with his infidelity. Is this a common occurrence, I ask myself and shake my head. I could never cheat on Barbie or any other woman for that matter. I'm not good at telling lies – my face goes bright red. And I couldn't do anything to a person that I'd hate being done to me. Therefore, the thought would never enter my tiny little brain.

I read on. Sheila, his long-suffering wife had worked in the ticket office at Durham train station before she retired, and Geoff had written this sentence in his notes which were Jack's own words.

'I don't mind looking after Sheila because it salves my conscience – it makes me feel better. She's stood by me from the day we married and deserves the best.

We have two foreign carers who I'm a little suspicious about and I hide her jewellery and purse when they're in the house.'

Jeez, I whistle through my teeth. People's lives are mega interesting. My stomach growls for lunch and I leave the office.

***

There's a long queue outside the nearby Jorvik Centre. It looks like a coach full of school children has landed with their teachers. The children are excited, and the teachers frazzled. One of them raises an eyebrow at me, and I smile. 'Hey kids, have a good time in there and don't let the Vikings get you!'

Everyone laughs as I pass by. It's an amazing museum which is always a stop on my historic tours.

I wander up towards the minster buying a Cornish pasty on route and sit outside in the early summer sunshine. It's a beautiful majestic structure and I watch tourists in awe upon seeing the minster for the first time. For me, it's somewhere I've visited many times and is part of our York landscape.

Today however, I'm deep in thought and remember how we've used the LNER train a few times to go from York up to Durham. However, I've never thought about train drivers before and their actual job of driving a train full of people every day. Is it monotonous? Does the responsibility of having the safety of people's lives in your hands weigh heavily? I remember reading how in train crashes there is always sympathy for the driver as well as the passengers who've suffered. It must be a traumatic experience.

I think of Jack pulling into the major stations on a daily basis and decide he'd been like airline pilots with a reputation for having a girl in each far-flung place they visit. However, I wouldn't have thought this of train drivers. Jack must have had escapades up and down the country in his hey-day.

I sigh knowing everyone has a past and something to hide. Like me I suppose, so I can't criticise Jack. And if making good afterwards counts as some type of forgiveness, then I reckon it can only be a good thing. I expect, in his own way, Jack is trying to make it up to Sheila by looking after her so well now.

Of course, for ninety year old Sergeant Riley it's the opposite because his wrongdoing had been confessed at the end of his life so he couldn't do this. Which makes me think, why hadn't he confessed earlier in his life to make amends? Possibly, he'd be frightened of repercussions with the army. And it wasn't something he'd want to shout from the rooftops in gratification. In fact, this transgression would have been shameful to say the least especially to other soldiers who'd won medals for bravery.

I'd heard the pride in Mrs Webster's voice when she spoke of the DLI. Their reputation, high standards, courage and professionalism would all come into question. And if this sergeant was a decent man, he would have felt humiliated by what he'd done.

I wonder if it had been a knee-jerk reaction when he shot Private Jones? Had he been completely out of control fighting in the throes of the battle and filled with rage when he saw the Private running away and leaving his comrades to suffer?

This would be totally understandable, or had he known exactly what he was doing, and it was pre-meditated. I imagine him after the war at home. Had he been remorseful and lived the rest of his life regretting what he'd done?

I sigh, this is something Jack will never know. I have to agree with his decision not to send the letter of apology. If the family knew what had happened in the war to their loved one, Private Jones it wouldn't help in any way. I know it's a modern expression to say people need closure, but this ending was so harrowing it's probably best not to know at all.

***

I wander back down to the office and make a coffee when a tingle on my mobile alerts me to a text. I smile seeing my friend's name, Simon. 'Hey, how's the new job going? Are you coming to the writing group tonight – do you want a lift?'

I'd met Simon last year and he's quickly become a very good friend. It's not that I'm a loner but have to admit I don't have many close friends. I have many acquaintances and work colleagues but not long term friends. I've never felt the need, being more than happy with my own company and that of my first wife, and now Barbie.

Also, I'm not a sporty man and don't have many interests other than writing which can be a solitary past time. Which is why I love our writing group so much. I'm amongst like-minded people and Simon is exactly the same. He too, lives for his wife, June and being an author. We exchange views, spark ideas of one another, and the group has a general feeling of camaraderie.

I reply, 'Yes, please - I'll be waiting, and the job is good so far. I'm writing up a really interesting case which is a deathbed confession??' I insert a smiley emoji.

Simon answers, 'Wow - that sounds amazing! Why not tell the group about it tonight – it might trigger some stimulating discussions.'

I think about this and the confidential issue but know I can talk about it without names and locations. 'Great idea – I'll do just that. See you later when I will reveal all!!'

Chapter Four

Simon Travis pulls up outside my house and I climb into the front of his red Nissan Micra. I smile and greet my friend in his usual woolly green sweater and brown corduroy trousers. In the eighteen months I've known Simon I have literarily not seen him dressed in anything other than this attire, winter and summer months alike. He has a choice of different coloured sweaters and trousers, so to call him fashion conscious would be an understatement.

'Hey, how's it going?'

Simon nods, 'Good thanks - just very busy now I've got a publisher.'

I glance at him while he's concentrating at the roundabout. Although the same age, Simon is three books ahead of my writing achievements, and I think he's one of the best new crime writers in the country. He's secured a traditional publisher for his latest novel and the offer includes another book which he's busy writing.

Simon has achieved what I'm longing to have – my books with a mainstream publisher. In my mind, self-publishing has been a great way to get off the starter blocks, but I'm now more than ready for the sprint race.

All of us in the writing group are delighted with his success, none more than me, and although he tends to play the book deal down, I know he's secretly cock-a-hoop. It's just like him to try and conceal his success, and not to boast about it.

I say, 'But that's a good thing – right?'

The big man smiles at me and nods. Other people would call him fat, but I prefer to use the word, stocky, it's much kinder. We'd had a Christmas meal together with Barbie and June who'd told me how Simon tries to hide his bulk in baggy sweaters. He's not much taller than me, but I think of him as a gentle giant as most friends would, until you read his novels. They're gruesome and shocking in equal measures and I often wonder how his characters depraved minds can create such grisly scenes.

Simon says, 'I'll not ask about the job as such because I know you're going to tell the group all about it later,' he says. 'But how's your book doing that is set in Durham?'

I shrug my shoulders. 'Okay, I guess, about thirty copies a month so far which could be better, I suppose.'

Simon taps his hands on the steering wheel as we sit at traffic lights heading down the bank into Harrogate centre. 'Well, for what it's worth I think it's a great story and the location is integral to the crime. I mean, Durham Cathedral and the castle is an amazing setting to have as a backdrop. And that sheer drop down to the river - well, it would be a great place to push someone over!'

I throw my head back and laugh. 'Ah, now you're talking.'

'No, but seriously,' he says. 'I love all your characters – they're brilliant.'

I grin and nod in appreciation. I know Simon struggles with his characters' personalities and is the first to admit that he finds interesting people difficult to imagine. Now I've got to know Simon, he's much more open in our friendship. When I'd first met him at the writing group, we'd all found him a little shy and introverted. He's definitely not, as Geoff called me, a people's person.

We pull into Harrogate Library car park and Simon turns off the ignition. Harrogate is the definitive boutique spa town in Yorkshire. There are usually events, concerts, and shows in The Royal Hall which is a beautifully restored Grade 11 listed theatre. Its thriving streets are always busy with shops and eateries and cultural events. We have a branch of "The Ivy" restaurants which are famous for what I call, posh-nosh and we've been a couple of times for celebratory meals. I'm partial to the Shepherd's Pie, which was Noel Coward's favourite in their London restaurant.

The old spa heritage can be seen at every turn in the centre from the Royal Pump Room Museum to The Turkish Baths where June works. I've been in the café and entrance once with Barbie and the art décor is quite simply stunning. Coloured tiles form archways which characterise the 1920s making it a peaceful atmosphere to enjoy spa treatments. It has a great reputation.

Simon turns to look at me and grabs his old, battered satchel from the back seat. 'I've a feeling tonight is going to focus on the author interviews session because it's only a few weeks away and Cynthia will want to plan everything to an inch of its life.'

I chortle and agree as we walk through the car park. I stand still and look at the beautiful Yorkshire stone building with huge pillars at the front framing a big old window. Above the window is carved into the stone, Carnegie Library.

At just before seven o'clock it's a lovely summer's evening and I don't relish sitting inside after being cooped up all day in the office. But knowing I'll enjoy the company of my fellow writers I put a spring in my step.

Along to my right, I see another group member, Angela Dobson negotiating her way on crutches through the main side door. I run to help by holding the doors wide open. Angela is in her early forties and has Multiple Sclerosis. She tells everyone, on a good day she can walk with crutches but on a bad day she is confined to her wheelchair. Her long blonde hair is tied up in a ponytail from her pale face. When we'd first met, she had cynically said, 'Oh, I've years of this ahead of me to look forward to.'

However, she'd said it with a broad smile on her face and over the months I've noticed she won't accept sympathy from any of us. Considering her condition, she's one of the most upbeat women I know, which is amazing. I don't think I'd be able to brave out her daily struggles like she does – I would probably be in the depths of despair. Only a few years ago she was running marathons and now she can barely walk. It must be crucifying for her to look at her life now to what it had been.

When I first met Angela, I hadn't been sure what MS was but found out on Google. It is a condition which affects the brain and spinal cord, causing a wide range of symptoms with vision, arm and leg movements, sensation or balance. It's a lifelong ailment that can cause serious or mild disability with a reduced life expectancy and is more common in women. From comments in the group, I know her husband is devoted to her and luckily for Angela, he is a physiotherapist.

Following her through the doors, I shake my head and tut in sadness. It seems so unjust that this disabling disease could afflict Angela – it's cruel to say the least. Simon follows us along the corridor as we all exchange pleasantries, but I see his brown hooded eyes downcast as though he's thinking the same as myself.

On a good session there's about thirty people in the writing group and we're all at various stages of our work. We meet every fortnight in the library from seven until nine and I love every minute of spending time in their company. The ground floor is vast with a mix of old, oak book shelves reaching up to the ceiling but with modern bright purple chairs and small tables.

There's a current notice board with posters covering numerous activities to be held in the library. Next to this is a section with beautiful old photographs of Harrogate. One, in particular, I love called, The Sun Colonnade, although there's no name of the photographer. It's a photograph of a long wide walkway where Victorian clad people stroll past others who are sitting in director-style chairs reading. Overhead is a huge wooden trellis which I suppose is to keep the sun from beating down on their heads.

We turn and head downstairs to the basement where there are three meeting rooms. The largest is called The Victoria Room where we hold our sessions. It easily sits twenty to thirty people around a long table down the centre of the room surrounded by more purple plastic chairs. There's a big screen in the corner for presentations, not that we've used this before.

I love all types of clubs and societies for reading or writing in groups. Of course, there's some obsessive followers like the Sherlock Holmes' fans, but my biggest pleasure in our small group is how we exchange thoughts and encourage each other. There's no internet involved – it's all about books, what we read and write.

 Which is the core value of the leader in our writing group and here she comes now, I think, as Cynthia Beauchamp sweeps through the room towards us. Cynthia always denies the fact that she is the leader of the group claiming we are all a team, but she is the founder member, and everyone treats her as such.

 I can usually smell Cynthia's strong musk perfume settle around me before I see her and reckon, she's in her late sixties. Simon calls her Boho-hip, but from the first day we met, she's reminded me of Miss Jones, played by Frances de la Tour in "Rising Damp". Not that I liken myself to Rigsby, of course.

 In her typical flowing silk kimono dress she seems to glide, not walk. I've never actually seen her hair because it's always encased in colourful turbans. Tonight, she's wearing a gold pleated turban with a huge bling brooch at the front. Cynthia is deeply passionate about the group and writes beautiful prose and short stories. Apparently, when she was younger, she performed in amateur dramatics and loved the stage. Which is obvious for anyone to see.

 'Ooh, darling,' she cries loudly. 'How lovely to see you.'

 I grin when she takes my arm and strokes it gently. We have this soft teasing camaraderie between us where she gives me the glad-eye, flirts flamboyantly, and I behave like David Niven. It's silly really and Barbie thinks I'm mad. I could be accused of stroking her ego, but I can tell flattery and attention makes her feel good. Which at the end of the day is harming no one. I often feel as though our little interludes are like a screentest for her. Cynthia once told me, she'd only ever felt alive when the spotlight was on her on stage or under the film cameras.

'Good evening, Cynthia,' I say, and lower my voice to her ear. 'Looking delectable, as ever...'

She has a throaty giggle and whispers back, 'And you brighten up the room as soon as you enter, dearest Clive.'

To others, Cynthia might have an unhinged look in her eyes and her mental state may come into question, but I think of her as simply highly strung. She pretends to be genuinely middle class, but I can tell she thinks of herself as upper middle class, if there is such a thing nowadays.

Simon told me she has a huge old property on Promenade Court, which is a side street up from Swan Lane and is worth mega-bucks, his words, not mine. As he used to be solicitor conducting the buying and selling of properties, I figure he knows what he's talking about.

It's a three story house where she lives with two cats and a lodger on the top floor. Her husband died many years ago but left her without money worries. Apparently, the lodger only pays a pittance in rent and has been there since her husband passed because she doesn't like living alone. She finds comfort in his company even if it's just the sound of his shoes on the stairs and him moving around above her.

We all help ourselves to coffee and I watch our Chinese lady who writes beautiful poetry carry a coffee to Angela. Her name is Fen, which apparently means, scent and her family are originally from Beijing. They've run a Chinese restaurant here for many years. In her mid-fifties, she wears silk, body-hugging dresses and often a matching shawl.

She'd had trouble two years ago with a few horrid comments in the town centre from narrow-minded bigots about the Covid Virus and how it had begun in China. We'd made it known that she had our total support and would help with any issues which occurred. I can neither believe nor try to understand people who are vindictive to our neighbours of different nationalities.

My belief is that the more diverse we are, the more interesting and cultured we become. Other nations with their own ethos have always fascinated me and I can almost picture myself in scenes when Fen reads beautiful poetry from her homeland. I'd like to say China is on my bucket list of places to visit but I don't think Barbie and I will ever have the finances to do this. Unless, I smile, I write the next best seller.

Now we are all settled in our chairs, Cynthia opens the session with local news and tells us how she'll go through the plans for our hosting of the author interview panel. We progress with some of our overly keen members who want to read their work out to the group.

'And now,' Cynthia says. 'Our darling Clive has started a new detective job this week and wants to captivate us all about a case he has resolved.'

She raises an eyebrow at me, and I stand up in front of everyone. I figure there's around thirty people here tonight and for some reason I never feel totally relaxed about speaking to an audience. I'm not sure where this comes from because I'm enthusiastic about my work, but

I rub the palms of my hands down my jeans and lick my dry lips.

'Well, that's very kind of you, Cynthia, but I'm not a detective and I am not solving cases,' I say. 'I'm merely an assistant for a PI and am writing up all the case notes he has recorded.'

I take a deep breath and launch into my story about the Sergeant who shot a Private during the war but told everyone it had happened down the country. I don't mention any names, of course, and speak in what I hope is a mysterious tone of voice with the dramatic outcome of cowardice.

There's utter silence while I'm talking and as I look around at everyone, I see they're hanging upon my every word. To use an old theatrical term, I have them in the palm of my hand. When I finish, I take a dramatic bow in the silence of the room then loud clapping ensues.

Fen stands up. Her jet black hair seems to swish while she moves her small head. She says quietly, 'Every good lie has a journey of truth.'

Angela leans over to Fen and says, 'Hey, is that a motto from a fortune cookie?'

I see Angela's smiling blue eyes and Fen squeezes her arm. 'No, it's a saying from my father who was an old, but very wise man.'

I have visions of Victorian opium dens and old Chinese men with long hair tied in a top-knot sitting cross-legged puffing on pipes to smoke the opium. I whisper this to Simon who laughs – we share the same sense of humour.

There's a great deal of discussion about the war before we all leave for the night. One elderly man who I think is called Dan approaches me as I'm gathering my notebook and papers together. He's not one of the regular writers which attend the group and I've never had a personal conversation with him before.

He tends to write stories about naval battles at sea which I think are monotonous, but Simon reckons he is a good writer. Each to their own, I suppose, and give him a big smile. 'Hey, there,' I say.

I'm expecting him to congratulate me about my story, but his bushy eyebrows knit together when he frowns, and his almost black eyes harden.

'You need to be careful about what you're saying to people,' he says. 'Not everyone is as they seem!'

I stand still and open my mouth to speak but don't get the chance.

He growls then shouts, 'My grandfather was a conscientious objector and suffered terribly during the war. He was in prison for years where he was harassed and beaten until the law changed and even then, when he was released, he was tormented in the community with white feathers!'

My mouth dries and I swallow hard. I can feel Simon behind me at my shoulder while I hold out my hand to Dan.

'Look, I feel terrible that I've upset you,' I say. 'I'm very sorry, but it wasn't my intention at all, and yes, I will be more careful in future.'

Dan ignores my outstretched hand, turns on his heel and strides away.

I look at Simon who shrugs. 'That's not your problem – it's his,' he says. 'You apologised but strictly speaking you didn't need to – it's not your fault about his grandfather.'

I nod. 'I know, but maybe I told the story in a cocky manner and should have been more sympathetic?'

Simon shakes his head. 'No, you weren't cocky, Clive,' he says. 'And the discussion afterwards by everyone was far more contentious where you didn't even comment.'

I follow him out of the room feeling flat even though up until Dan's outburst we'd had a good meeting. However, I console myself with the fact that above all, Simon is a fair man and if I'd been out of line he would have said so. Simon offers me a lift home so we can swap tips for social media, and I brighten determined to put the outburst behind me.

As we walk to the car, I remember the celebration we'd had on the night when Simon had received his offer from the publisher. We'd had to take a taxi home because it was such a late night and Simon had been worse for wear with champagne.

I can't help wondering if my time will ever come to receive an offer from a publisher. Just thinking about it makes my stomach churn with excitement – it would be such a massive achievement. I grin, knowing I have to persevere and put in the hard work because seeing my books on a shelf in Waterstones would be a dream come true.

Chapter Five

The following week Geoff rings when I'm in the office. I tell him, 'I've finished writing up the soldiers deathbed confession so is there any order for the others?'

'Yeah,' he says. 'Can you do the search I did for a missing brother - I think he was called Jake Robinson.'

There's quite a lot of noise on the call and it sounds to me as though he's in a bar with loud music playing. I raise my voice a little. 'Yeah, sure.'

Geoff shouts, 'I basically want to know if Jake died in hospital because that's where I found him. He'd been admitted with severe hepatitis, and they hadn't thought he would survive. If he died, then we can close the job down. The contact was from his sister Rose and her mobile number will be there somewhere,' he says. 'Can you ring her and ask what happened to her brother?'

I agree and hear a female voice shout in the background. 'Ooooh, Geoff!'

I wonder if that is Jemma? It's often a curse to have a suspicious mind and smile when Geoff ends the call.

This is not going to be an easy conversation with Rose but ultimately part of the job. I pull back my shoulders and set my jaw firm. If I'm going to do this role, and do it well, I have to be able to complete all the tasks even the difficult ones. I begin to read the initial notes from a twenty-four year old woman, Rose Jackson who lives in Knaresborough. She'd asked Geoff to trace her brother who'd been sleeping rough in Manchester.

I take a deep breath and dial her number. It rings for a while, and I wait for an answer machine to pick up. Then suddenly a breathless voice answers.

'Hello.'

I introduce myself and say, 'Rose, I just wanted to ask what has been the outcome with your brother in the hospital?'

Her voice is shaky, and it sounds as though she's been crying, or is ready to burst into tears now. 'W…well,' she says, and takes in a noisy deep breath.

I wait patiently and surmise her brother is no longer alive. 'It's fine,' I say. 'Just take your time - I feel awful having to ask.'

Rose begins to sob loudly. And I wait. Perhaps my empathy has made her worse and I should have used a brisk non-committal tone as Geoff probably would have done. But that's not my style.

She blows her nose.

And still I wait.

'S…Sorry,' she says. 'Jake went ten days ago.'

Now I'm floundering because she'd said he went. Does that mean he died or went somewhere else – another hospital unit, or back to street life? I frown. If I use the word die and he hasn't, it'll be a reprieve. But if Jake has died then at least I'll know and put Rose out of the misery having to repeat herself.

'Okay,' I say, and relax my shoulders. 'Did Jake die in the hospital or at home with you?'

I hear her sigh heavily and breathe out loudly. 'Sorry, it's just some days I can get the word d…died out of my mouth but then sometimes I can't - it's still too raw!'

I feel dreadfully sorry for Rose and my heart squeezes for this poor woman. I think about the police on TV detective shows and the same sentence they use with grief-stricken people. I ask, 'Rose, are you on your own?

Is there anyone that can come to be with you –
neighbours or friends?'

'No, but thanks,' she says. 'They were here all of
yesterday because it was the funeral, but today I just
wanted to be on my own.'

Now, I know it was a bad time to ring and maybe could
have left it a couple of days, but as Mrs Webster often
says, 'It's a shame we don't have a crystal ball in life to
see ahead of what's coming at us.' And she's right.

Rose has stopped crying now and I figure her voice is
more stable. 'Ah, I see, and you've no other family?'

'Nooo,' she cries. 'Our little sister, Daisy died years
ago.'

Her voice seems to crack up again at the mention of
Daisy. My heart sinks even further and all I can mutter
is, 'Oh, dear.'

Geoff hasn't told me to go and talk to her and might
even be annoyed if I do so, but I feel I have to go, in
other words, I want to see her. Barbie is home tonight
from work and Knaresborough will be a nice day out for
us both.

Quickly, I decide and say, 'Look Rose, I feel terrible
that I've upset you by ringing to ask about Jake, so could
I come and see you?'

I hear her take in a deep sigh of relief. She says, 'Oh,
would you? There's something more that's happened,
and I don't know what to do about it.'

My ears prick up now. 'Of course, I'll help anyway I
can, although Geoff is way more experienced than I am.'

'No,' she says. 'I'd planned to come and see Geoff in a
few weeks' time when I'd got myself together a bit

more, but I would much rather talk to you than come into York like I did last time.'

Gold star for me, I think and smile at her compliment. I'm not sure how Geoff will take this, but that concern is for another day. 'Okay, how about tomorrow around one o'clock?'

She agrees and I hang up feeling a mixture of intrigue and relief that I'll get the chance to find out what's happened after Jake's demise.

I make a strong coffee and wonder whether I should tell Geoff I'm going to see Rose. Afterall, he did say at the interview I could get more involved with cases if I wanted to, and in this situation, I do. As he's still in Scotland, and may well advise against seeing Rose, I decide to tell him when he returns. This way, I'll have been and will have more information. Plus, I think sipping the hot coffee, it may create more work for us, and in effect, more service charge for him.

Yes, I think happily, a day out to Knaresborough tomorrow will be lovely, and for Barbie too. There's a certain boutique shop she likes in the town centre, and I feel our credit card give a gentle squeeze.

When I leave for the day, I wonder what I'll find when I get there tomorrow with Rose and if I can get her to open up more about Jake.

Chapter Six

We've set off to Knaresborough in Barbie's car. The sun is peeping behind a big cloud and I'm hoping to reach Rose by one o'clock. I glance at Barbie driving in a white sleeveless dress. Her eyes are shining as is her blonde bobbed hair. We'd had such a great night together sharing pizza and loving each other in our big bed. Whoever wrote the saying, absence makes the heart grow fonder, has it bang-on. I hate it when she heads off to work and is away from home but love it when she returns.

We are driving on the A59 and usually the journey takes around thirty minutes. When Barbie pulls up at a junction, she gives me a little smile. It's coquettish as though she is remembering last night, too. She often does this and would give strangers the impression it's all part of her gentle loving personality. Which it is, but there's another side to Barbie, especially in the bedroom that blows my mind - she's like a panther waiting to pounce. I'm just glad the leap, when it happens is onto me. It's one of the things, of which there are many, that I love about her. She gives you more than you're expecting all of the time and not just in our bed.

We find a parking space easily and both agree the town seems relatively quiet. Knaresborough is a warren of medieval streets that weave their way up and down the hill. The town centre is perched on the cliffs above River Nidd and the railway viaduct above is an imposing sight.

We've been a few times before so decide not to do the touristy bits but can't help looking down onto the river and small cluster of stone houses built into the side – it's a beautiful sight and I sigh in pleasure.

'Phew, this still takes my breath away,' I say and drape my arm along her shoulder. She hugs me and nods in agreement. As if it was pre-planned, a blue Northern train chugs along the top of the viaduct which adds to the perfection of the view.

'Right,' I say. 'I'll head off to find Rose's cottage and text you later where we can meet up?'

She winks. 'And I'll head off for a coffee and then the shops.'

***

The address is Cheapside, which is near the centre, and I set off walking briskly. Cheapside reminds me of an area in London from Barbie's favourite film, "Pride & Prejudice" which believe me, we've watched a few times now. I often fall asleep mid-way and receive a nudge in the ribs from her. Of course, Cheapside in London back then was a nice area but not good enough for Mr Darcy's snobby family.

As I approach the row of cottages, I can tell that Cheapside here in Knaresborough is the same – not cheap at all. The cottages are built with light-polished, Yorkshire stone and are small with different coloured wood doors. Rose's door is duck-egg blue with white vintage-style windows and the usual old high step.

I tap on the door, and it swings open immediately which makes me think Rose was waiting on the other side. I smile at the young woman in front of me and put out my hand to shake.

Rose is very thin and tall. She's wearing a floral maxi dress in bright pink. A matching headband is on her forehead keeping her long black hair from her face. Four long chain necklaces fall onto the dress with three gold bangles on her wrist. I remember Simon's comment at the writing group about Boho-hippy and know this is Rose's style.

'Hi,' she says and smiles. 'Come in and make yourself comfortable.'

I step straight into a small lounge which is very blue. It's trendy but with original period features of an old fireplace, woodburning stove, and two column radiators. The large velour sofa, walls, carpet and curtains are all different shades of blue and I know Barbie would be in raptures about this décor.

I sit on the royal-blue sofa, and she sits opposite me in a pale blue occasional chair. I look around and place my iPad onto a big glass coffee table.

'You can tell I like the colour blue,' she says and grins. It's an impish face that doesn't quite work with her long hair. Not that I'm an expert in these things, but I reckon a short haircut would suit her much better.

She offers me coffee and scurries off down a hallway into the kitchen. I look out of the big window at the back of the room and into the sizeable garden. I spot her green bicycle propped up against, yes, you've guessed it, a blue shed. The bicycle has a basket on the front, and I see a small kitten poking its head over the wicker.

Rose hurries back into the lounge asking if I want milk and sugar and when I answer she scuttles back again. Does she ever walk at a normal pace, I wonder, or does she always run around like this. I hope I'm not making her nervous and try to put her at ease.

Settled with a mug of coffee, I ask, 'So, do you work in Knaresborough, Rose?'

She nods and sits back in her chair a little although her shoulders are still hunched. 'Oh, yes, I'm a librarian and have worked in our library for three years now – it's just on the market place.'

I glance over to the books on an old shelf and can tell she's an avid reader. They look like romance stories with a wide selection of Mills and Boon, which I figure will all have happy ever after endings.

She's follows my gaze. 'They're pure escapism, not that my life will ever be that way, but it's light-hearted reading in which I can lose myself.'

I nod and hoping to relax her more I talk about something she knows well and launch into my pitch about my books on Amazon. It works. She drinks her coffee, crosses her ankles clad in brown suede boots and sits right back in the chair. We have a lengthy discussion about eBooks verses paperbacks and the value of libraries in our community. Rose's eyes have brightened, and she now has an animated look on her face. I know she's engaged in our conversation.

I've always had the impression that librarians were demure, gentle souls who love their jobs because books are the most important things in their lives. A little like authors, I think and smile. However, with the modernisation of many local libraries, the old-fashioned appearance has long since gone. Older ladies in checked suits with rimmed glasses perched on the end of their noses shouting, quiet please, are a thing of the past.

Now, the younger librarians are abreast in modern methods of reading, IT and organising groups of people. I think of our library in Harrogate where we gather for the writing group and know Rose will display all their activities in a modern what's-on format. Children's activities, rightly so, figure high in priority of the facilities in libraries. I'd once heard a children's book author say that getting young people to read books was paramount.

I decide it's time now to get to the reason for visiting. 'Have you always lived here?' I ask, 'And if it doesn't upset you too much again can you tell me a little about your family and Jake.'

I learn that their parents were divorced, and Jake had left his dad to live on the streets with £4K in his bank account. His father gave him the money from the share of the family home after it was sold even though he knew Jake would spend it all on booze and drugs. Their father had bought an apartment in Spain and moved there with a parting shot to Jake, 'Don't ever ask for more money because you won't get it!'

Their mother bought a small flat in Alnwick and quickly remarried. Rose had made her new job in Knaresborough library the reason to leave Alnwick, but really it was because she didn't like the new step father her mother had chosen. He was mean and grumpy.

Rose nods. 'Yeah, I'm sorry about yesterday on the phone but it just sweeps over me, and to answer your question, no, I was brought up in Morpeth, Northumberland. There was Mam, Dad, Jake, me and little Daisy. We had a biggish house near the river where we all played. I loved it,' she says, looking out of the window with a wistful expression in her eyes.

I nod and smile to encourage her to keep talking.

'I've missed my little sister, Daisy, from the day she drowned in the river,' she says. 'Mam said I was the typical middle-child always craving attention but looking back, I don't think I was.'

I frown. I don't have siblings, so struggle to think how life would be different if I hadn't been alone in my childhood and I tell her this.

Rose smiles. 'Well, it can be a hinderance at times, but I loved Jake and Daisy dearly. After Daisy drowned, Mam and Dad were never the same again and when they split up, of course, I stayed with Mam, but Jake went with Dad to Manchester at first. It was a devastating wrench because I'd followed Jake around hero-worshipping him from being little. He was kind, caring, and knew everything we needed to know. We made up games and competitions of which he often let me win.'

She stops and takes a deep breath as if the memories are torturous to recap. 'However, on that fateful day, Mam had taken me into Newcastle to choose a bridesmaid dress. We were planning for a cousins wedding and Dad was taking Jake for a new suit the week after. Daisy already had her toddler's dress which was a gift from our grandma who'd made it to fit. Whereas, aged twelve I wanted something more fashionable. For years afterwards I'd tortured myself wishing we hadn't gone.'

I lean forward. 'Rose, if this is too painful, we can leave it for a few weeks until you've pulled yourself together – it might be easier?'

She shakes her head. 'No, Clive, I'll keep going and get this all out now so we can move forwards.'

'Jake started using drugs at an early age, or so my dad always said. And by the time he was sixteen he'd left Dad and was living on the streets in Manchester,' Rose says, and takes another deep breath. 'Then he was in prison for a few years, and although my parents disowned Jake, I never gave up on him. I hadn't believed all the bad things everyone said about him and his dodgy reputation, so I sent him money every month. Even though I knew he would probably spent it on drugs. I couldn't bear to see him with nothing. And then he disappeared so I contacted Geoff to see if he could find him in Manchester.'

I rub my chin listening to this tragic tale. 'Gosh, that must have been so hard for you, Rose.'

She nods. 'It was, and when Geoff found him in the hospital I dashed straight to his bedside. He was in a side room and looked dreadful. I hadn't see him for years but would have recognised his green eyes anywhere. He was surrounded with drips, and tubes, and an oxygen mask, and I couldn't believe the yellow-tinged skin was of my good-looking brother.'

I sigh. 'And were you on your own?'

She nods and waves her hand a little so the gold bangles jingle together. 'Neither of my parents would come to see him – they were too ashamed even when the doctors said he wouldn't last another day.'

I shake my head in disbelief. 'It's terrible that no one in the hospital could help – didn't they have a priest or someone who could have sat with you?'

'Well, yes, a lay-preacher called into the room the day he died and held my hand. But it was what Jake said before he died that's tortured me ever since.'

I sit back on the sofa. 'Tell me,' I say.

'Well, Jake was mumbling and at times I wasn't even sure if he recognised me but then he grabbed my hand

and said, 'Rose, our little Daisy didn't drown in the river - I held her down under the water!'

I gasp loudly and then mutter an apology. It was an inconsiderate thing to do but the shock had reverberated around my mind.

While my brain is trying to work through this, she continues. 'Jake had always been terribly jealous of Daisy and all the baby attention she got but I still can't believe this of him,' she says. 'And I know, I've been accused of seeing him through rose-tinted glasses in the past, excuse the pun, but he was very clever and excelled in maths and science at school. He organised games for us, and I know he loved me, but maybe not so much, Daisy because he was jealous of her and the care she received. When she was born, he was the eldest of three, not two, and everything seemed to change. I know I'm defending him yet again, but I mean, he couldn't have d…done it - could he?'

Her eyes fill with tears again and I pray she isn't going to cry. I can't handle people crying, especially women. I never know what to say or do. It's at this stage, I wished I'd brought Barbie with me as she'd suggested. Barbie could have hugged Rose which as a man and a stranger, I can't do.

Rose asks, 'Clive, do you think the drugs they were giving him to prolong his life had sent him a bit crazy? Perhaps, he was delirious and didn't know what he was saying?'

'Well, it's a possibility - did he say anymore?'

She nods and wipes her wet eyes with a tissue. 'Yes, he told me how it had happened. Apparently, Daisy had fallen into the river, and he had ran to her. He'd slumped to his knees on the edge of the river and tried to grab her yellow cardigan. She'd been crying and flaying around which annoyed him, so he pushed her back under to stop her screeching. Everything in his head had turned bright red and the next thing he knew was Dad yelling and running towards them. Jake said that Dad had thrown his head back and howled like a wolf, and then there was a load of hullabaloo with sirens and ambulances.'

I shake my head again. 'Well, I don't know if he was capable of doing this, Rose,' I say. 'But it certainly seems as though Jake has a clear memory of the incident and the river on that day.'

'Yeah, but could it have just been a dream or something he'd seen on TV and in his confused state he thought it was real?'

I can tell she's grasping at straws and desperate for me to agree that her brother couldn't possibly have done this. However, I set my brain into gear and think through the scenario piece by piece.

Rose says wistfully, 'I remember reading in a book somewhere which said children usually live up to what you believe of them, and I know Dad was often tough on him. Jake was always looking for his approval and strived to achieve his recognition but never did. I've thought it through repeatedly since he died and know if Jake hadn't done this to Daisy, then my family wouldn't have been split in two. We would all have lived together happily ever after. And I've also wondered, if it was true then maybe that's why Jake started drinking and taking drugs?'

I nod and say, 'It could be, Rose, can you remember if Daisy had a yellow cardigan?'

She throws her head back and begins to sob loudly.
'Yes, yes, she did!'

Chapter Seven

I'm in the office again today and Geoff is out somewhere on his travels. I open Rose's folder and decide to recap over the Knaresborough visit and write my own account of her details. If Geoff does refer this case to the police for further investigation and the verdict from 2002 is re-opened, my notes will play an important role.

I learn from research how many confessions involve an admittance of a crime the dying have committed which obviously cannot be prosecuted once they have passed. However, another use for a deathbed confession in the criminal justice system is to re-open a case which has gone cold to gain closure for the victim's family and friends, even if prosecution is not an option. This, I decide will be a decision for the authorities and not me, nor Geoff for that matter.

I had left Rose crying in her cottage and told her to ring me when she felt better. Pathetic, I know, but dealing with women in upsetting situations is not something I'm very good at. I'd wandered back down into the town centre whistling the song, "My Brother Jake" and then scolded myself for being so crass at the time of someone's grief. However, this case was equally as interesting, if not more so than the soldier confession, because it was still active.

I'd rang Barbie and we'd arranged to meet down by the river. We had a picnic lunch and laid on the grass while I told her everything about Rose and Jake. I knew I could trust Barbie with confidential details and had always valued her opinion.

She'd said, 'Well, I suppose we all want to make a clear breast of our wrongdoings before we die, and I think I would want too as well. Not that I've drowned someone in a river, of course, but in another way it's a selfish act to heap grief and turmoil onto relatives and loved ones about misdemeanours just to give yourself a clear conscience. And, if you're religious the person may believe they'll be forgiven by a higher power before they die, allowing them entrance to heaven, especially after death.'

Now, I write this in my notes. I figure Jake must have had serious mental health issues both as a child and an adult to commit such a crime. I recall the Jamie Bulger case from years ago and how the two boys who'd tortured and killed the toddler had been teenagers like Jake. Surely, you'd have to be a little unbalanced to even think of this, let alone do it, or just downright evil, if there is such a thing.

Daisy would have been twenty-two now, if she'd lived and it's obvious Rose is in complete denial when it comes to Jake. As Mrs Webster would say, 'Rose is as soft as muck when it comes to her brother.'

And yes, as Rose had thought, drowning your sister was enough to drive anyone to alcohol and drugs. Jake probably used the addictions to block out his horrific memories. If I put myself into his mind, I'd probably want to die young rather than live to an old age with these dreadful thoughts forever in my mind. I reckon he must have had a serious and dangerous psychological disorder which experts reckon is now changing because of the way we live our lives.

There again, I can't imagine a person's state of mind who would want to sleep out on the streets. It's freezing cold in the winter, and all year around you're in danger of an attack. Of course, some street people prefer the freedom more than living in a hostel where constraints to conform are placed upon them. I'm afraid, I like my home comforts too much to even think of street life as a preference, but there again, I haven't lived Jake's life and am not in a place to criticise. As the old saying goes, I haven't walked a mile in his shoes.

Rose, I can tell, is too kind-hearted for her own good and unable to see the wickedness in people. By the way she scuttles about, she appears nervous and is obviously the type of woman to worry about things that have yet to happen. Rose seems generous to a fault and would make the best friend in the world to anyone she knows. I bet her kitten is spoilt rotten, too. However, as we have two cats, I know it's very hard not to do this. Barbie is like this with our cats, Spot and Stripe.

I make coffee and wonder if the police will re-open the case where Daisy's death had been recorded as misadventure. And if they do, what would this revelation mean to Rose? She's admitted that she couldn't go through all of the upset again especially being estranged from her parents. And if they wouldn't go to their own son's funeral, would they even be interested in this news?

Wandering over to the window I look down at people on the street below. What kind of parents were they? Once again, my suspicious mind kicks-in and I wonder, did they know Jake had drowned Daisy?

Did they cover it up for his sake and the scandal in Morpeth? And, had this been the main cause of their marital breakup?

The door to the office opens and I swing around in surprise expecting to see Geoff, but a woman breezes inside, and I hurry across the room to greet her. This lady is tall and stick thin wearing long white trousers which make her legs seem endless. Her face is pleasant enough, but to be kind, no one could say she was a good looking woman.

'Hello,' she says. 'I was hoping someone would be here.'

I introduce myself and lead her to a seat where she sits down crossing her legs in a comfortable manner. It's almost as though she knows her way around the office and has been here before. Could this be Jemma? But no, I shake my head, there's no trace of a Scottish accent in her voice.

I offer her a drink which she refuses with the brisk shake of her head. I sit down opposite and link my fingers together on top of the desk. 'So, how can I help you?'

Her glasses are two-tone frames with green on the top matching her small beady eyes and brown on the bottom which tones in with her short hair. I notice her mouth is turned down as if she's permanently scowling.

She asks, 'I'm just wondering if you do any surveillance work on your own?'

I'm confused and don't understand what she means. Does she want me to do something behind Geoff's back? I stare at her and ask, 'On my own?'

Nodding, she tries to smile which lessens the scowl to some degree. I get the feeling smiling isn't something she does on a regular basis.

She leans forward. 'You know, on the side as it were, so the boss doesn't know about it?'

I frown wondering where this is going. 'Er no, this business belongs to Geoff Smithson, not me.'

She looks down and twists her wedding ring around her finger. 'Yes, I know, but is surveillance something you would take on yourself? I'll pay you very well, how about £500 to follow my husband on Saturday?'

I gulp and then take a swig of coffee to play for time while I think about the proposition. She looks back up at me and I decide she has a cold and distant demeanour. There's no friendliness in her whatsoever. This, of course, could be because she's upset and worried about her marriage, or the total opposite for all I know.

'I know he's cheating on me and I want to know who the other woman is,' she says. 'I've found the usual cliché of receipts for hotels and restaurants in his jacket pocket, and to put it delicately, he hasn't ventured over to my side of the bed for months now.'

I wince at the open account of their intimate side of marriage, but already, apart from the amount of money which would be amazing towards our wedding fund, I know it's not for me. I shake my head. 'Em, well, it's a good offer thank you, but no, it's not something I'd like to do at this stage.'

She edges to the front of the chair. 'Aaah, are you sure I can't tempt you? Maybe with more money?'

I shake my head again more firmly this time. 'No, but I could check Geoff's diary for Saturday and ring him to see if he'll do it for you.'

'Ha!' She snorts and lurches up from the chair. Crossing her arms over her slight chest, she twists her thin lips. 'There's not much point in doing that because it's my husband, Geoff, who I want the surveillance on!'

'What?' I shout in shock. My stomach tightens and I feel my cheeks flush in the knowledge this is Geoff's wife, Margaret. Phew, that was a close call. If I hadn't had my wits about me, I could have fallen into her devious trap.

She stands in front of me now looking weary. It's the only word I can find to describe the expression on her face. It's almost as though she's at the end of her tether. There's a part of me that can't help feeling sorry for her, but I'm annoyed at the way she's done this in his office. Why didn't she introduce herself when she got here? And no wonder she knew the office layout, she'll have been here many times with her husband.

Lowering her head, she ambles slowly to the door. 'Well, I suppose it's good to see you're loyal to my husband, although God knows he doesn't deserve it, Clive.'

I get up to follow her. 'I'm sorry I can't help you, Mrs Smithson.'

Knowing I can't bite the hand that feeds me, as it were, and apart from this, I couldn't go behind Geoff's back. I like to think I'm more honest than this woman is, although not as clever perhaps, depending upon which way you look at it, but certainly not as deceitful.

She tuts and turns to me. 'Take care of yourself,' she says. 'And watch your back because Geoff is a perpetual liar – he can't seem to stop himself.'

I don't know what to say but try to give her a reassuring smile.

As a parting shot, she says, 'It was one of the reasons he was finished from the force along with dodging dealings and accepting bribery. Although he'd never admit to that, and of course, it was twenty years ago when the police force was very different.'

At this, she scurries out of the door, lets it bang shut and I hear her heels clattering down the stairs.

I sit back at the desk and run my hands through my hair. What have I got myself into by working here? And is it true about Geoff? I take a deep breath and try to calm myself into a more rational state of mind.

With such an authoritative voice, I figure, he had to be a policeman and wonder why this hadn't dawned upon me from the start. I can imagine him in a police station as the desk sergeant shouting at people, 'Sit down and be quiet!'

Sighing, I wonder if the dodgy dealing comment is right? I know he's already paid my wages for the work I've done so far, therefore, that's not a concern. And I haven't known him long enough to judge his character for the other accusation of being a liar. I think of Margaret and guess she's a good ten years older than Geoff. Cynically, I wonder if Margaret's money made her more attractive when they first married.

Although there's an hour to go before the end of the shift, I'm longing to see my lovely Barbie. And, it's been agreed I can work from home, if need be, so I print off three spreadsheets, fold them up into my bag and head for home.

Chapter Eight

When I walk through the front door, I inhale a delicious smell and know Barbie is cooking. 'Hi, sweetheart,' I call, and head through our small but cosy lounge.

Before Barbie arrived, it had been an empty square room with scuffed white walls, the sofa, a bookcase and TV in the corner. However, over the last couple of years she has improved the room by painting it cream and hanging new curtains with a subtle contrasting wallpaper over the fireplace. We have numerous photographs in chrome frames of her, well, my family now.

Mrs Webster has certainly taken me into the family nest. I smile at the photographs from our first Christmas with my soon to be, brother and sister-in-law, niece and nephew. Our warm home is full of Barbie's generous loving spirit now.

Taking pride of place on the back wall is a painting given to us by our art dealer friend, Rodger who is head of the neighbourhood watch committee. He'd been so grateful when I'd helped with a spate of burglaries in the area and retrieved most of the neighbours prized possessions, that he'd gifted the painting to us. It depicts a beach in Thailand and the shades of blue in the sea, and white sand with overlapping palm trees always makes me smile.

I head into our red kitchen. We call it the red kitchen because quite simply, it is red. It was the last addition to the house that my ex-wife had installed, and although Barbie isn't keen, and I've hated it from day one, we are living with it for now. The two long counter tops and cupboard fronts are shiny red with trendy chrome handles.

We have a breakfast bar with two high stools, which, yes, are red too. I stand in the doorway and watch her roll pastry on a board with a wooden rolling-pin.

She looks up, sees me and grins. 'Hey, what are you doing home early?'

I don't answer but hurry to her and wrap my arms around her waist pulling her into my hips. She's warm and smells as delicious as the pastry, which is the total opposite to Margaret in the office, and something I'll be eternally grateful for. Barbie hasn't changed whatsoever in the three years I've known her. I wonder if Margaret had been friendly and welcoming when Geoff first met her, and she's only became cold and distance because of his cheating and affairs.

Barbie swings around and wraps her floury hands around the back of my neck. 'Oooh, it's good to see you and a lovely surprise.'

I kiss down the side of her neck and the urge to join us together in a more natural form sweeps through my body. I murmur into her ear. 'How long is that pastry going to take?'

She giggles. 'Well, short crust pastry can settle better in the fridge for ten minutes if that's long enough for you?'

I throw my head back and laugh out loud. I put my arms under her legs, pick her up and carry her though to the lounge then toss her onto our slouchy sofa. I drop down on top of her, and you can guess the rest.

Later, I munch into a sausage roll straight from the oven and sigh in pleasure while Barbie cleans down the red counter top. I explain about Margaret's visit and Geoff's definite infidelity.

'Well, definite as far as Margaret is concerned,' Barbie says. 'But you must remember everyone is innocent until proved guilty. However, I do think you've done the right thing and it's best not to get involved with their domestic issues.'

I nod. 'True, and of course, I hardly know him. It would be different if I'd known him for years to judge his character, but I don't.'

Barbie climbs up on the stool opposite to me and cuts a sausage roll in half. 'Hmm, so in essence, we need to know if he is a liar, and did he get sacked from the police force for dodgy dealings?'

My mind races at her words - we need to know. Whenever I hear this, I automatically think of a way to discover the truth. Maybe that's the downfall of having a suspicious mind and know I can't let it be. 'Well yes, maybe I can think of a way to try and find more out about Geoff, on the QT of course.'

I wander back into the lounge and clear a space on top of our dining table in the corner of the room. If I could find out for definite that Geoff is cheating on Margaret, then at least I'll know what kind of guy I'm dealing with. Of course, if he is guilty, I've no intention of telling Margaret nor taking a penny from her. I frown and rub my chin with the need to know.

Placing the spreadsheets out flat on the table, I begin to read through Geoff's incomings and outgoings for the business.

Barbie follows me into the lounge and looks over my shoulder. 'Does Geoff know you're looking at these?'

I shrug. 'Well, they're in a public folder for anyone to read. It's not as if they've been saved into a private document that only he has access to enter.'

Barbie squeezes my shoulder. 'Just be careful, Clive because I know what you're like when you get a bee in your bonnet about something – but this time you might get your tail stung!'

I pat her hand when she heads towards the stairs.

'I'm going up to have a long soak in the bath,' she says.

I smile and continue tracing entries on the spreadsheets which all seem kosher. His tax is paid by an accountant. His expenses are all noted. His salary, and now mine, is entered in the correct columns, so as far as I can see, it's all above board. Of course, I'm no expert at how you would hide money in a business or receive money from dubious sources as a bribe for information and services, but I can't pick out any anomalies. I scrunch the papers up and toss them into the bin.

Maybe Geoff was a good cop catching bad corrupt cops? Or could he have been one of these policemen who broke the rules in the service of doing good? I sigh knowing if we didn't have the police then vigilantes could take over communities like they did in Bristol with mob rule.

Of course, Margaret could had made these accusations through jealousy, hurt, and embarrassment. She could have been lashing out and looking for ways to wreak havoc on Geoff in revenge after carrying a grudge. I've read about women who have cut up their husband's clothes or trashed their cars to ruin the man's beloved items. This brings the film, "The First Wives Club" with Goldie Hawn into my mind.

I smile, so perhaps, spreading lies about Geoff is Margaret's way of getting a sense of justice from their broken marriage.

I shrug. It would be good to know exactly who I'm working for, and maybe I should have done this before attending the interview. Yes, Geoff is well-dressed, suave, and comes across as a man-about-town, but is this just a smoke screen to the real man underneath? Is he involved in crime and underhand dealings, and is the PI business a façade?

I suppose the general impression of private investigators is not high up on the list of prodigious occupations. I think of TV programmes like, "Strike", "Magnum" and "Columbo". The main men in these programmes are what I'd call characters with flaws and none of them are like squeaky clean police officers.

Perhaps, a large proportion of PIs come into the business from the force because cases, like Rose and Jake's, are carried out through investigating people and situations. Both professions use the same set of detecting skills.

I Google his name and figure if Geoff has committed a major crime in the police force, then posts will come up associated with his name. But they don't – there's nothing. There is only Geoff's registered business on Companies House.

Next, I check him out on social media. There's no account on Facebook, nor Twitter, nor Instagram. So, I muse, as Mrs Webster would say, 'He obviously likes to keep his cards close to his chest'. Thinking now of her daughter, I mount the stairs quickly and call out to Barbie, 'Hey, is there room in that tub for me?'

Chapter Nine

Geoff is only here for the morning in the office as he has a meeting this afternoon in Leeds. We have coffee and a catch up while he walks around looking at the filing cabinet and new order on the shelves.

He grins. 'Hey, this is great! I'll actually be able to see what I'm looking for now.'

I pull my shoulders back and nod. I feel my ears going pink at his praise and know this is at least one tick in the box. He's my new boss and doesn't know me like the staff in the travel agency where I've worked for years, and the tour company owner.

I hand him the brown folder with, Sergeant Riley, written on the front. Geoff sits at his desk, and I busy myself putting leaflets and papers in order. I'm spying at him over the top of my computer while he has his head down reading the notes I've written.

'Yes, Clive, this is first-rate work. You've put my scribbles into a more orderly layout,' he says, and then sighs heavily. 'Having a structure in life is the one thing I've never been good at.'

I raise an eyebrow not sure where he's going with this and whether I should probe deeper. But now I've had a second tick in the box, I don't want to spoil my run of approval. Earlier, I'd thought of not telling him that I had been out to see Rose at home. However, deception isn't my way of doing things and as I've said before I'm not good at telling lies. So, I drain my coffee and brace myself.

I explain about the telephone call with Rose and how upset she'd been. 'And as Barbie wanted to go to Knaresborough shopping, I called into her cottage.'

I hand him another brown folder with, Jake Robinson on the front.

Geoff nods and once again begins to read. When he gasps, I know he's reached the place which states that Jake had drowned Daisy in the river.

I tap my trainers together under the desk wishing Geoff was a quicker reader because I'm longing to know what he thinks.

'The yellow cardigan is a good shout, Clive, well spotted. And I reckon we'll have to let the police and coroner know about this. We owe it to the parents whether they care about Daisy's death or not. I'm sure Rose will understand in time that it was necessary to do this,' he says. 'Give her a ring and let her know I'm referring the matter to the police now and then we can move onto our next case.'

I nod. Geoff's mobile rings and he looks down at the screen. 'Excuse me, I'll need to take this call,' he says, and strides out of the office.

In TV programmes, PIs seem to have strained relationships with the police, and I wonder if this is true with Geoff? Does he have old friends in the force who he contacts? Or does he simply contact whichever Inspector is on duty for the day?

I slope over to the window and see him downstairs on the street in his grey suit flinging his arm around with a look of consternation on his face. It's obvious he's arguing with someone. I wonder if it's Jemma or Margaret?

Geoff returns with his calm appearance back in place looking totally unruffled. 'So, Clive, would you like to take this new case I accepted yesterday?'

I stand up and hurry across to his desk. My senses are heightened, and a lightness fills my chest. Along with the excitement of a possible new crime to solve, I'm delighted Geoff is placing his trust in me to delve into the cases.

'Yeah, I'd love that.'

Geoff smiles. 'Great, it's about a happening from way back in 2007 which we now know is not what it seemed at the time.'

My antennae are back on red-alert, and I smile. 'Oh, right, this sounds mysterious.'

Geoff swings around to face me and hands over a printed email. 'This is all I have so far. It's from a girl called Sherrie Williams who is paying me to look at the case because her boyfriend, Michael has slight learning difficulties and can't do it himself. She's concerned about her partner, Michael Davies. I'm repeating the name Davies because you might remember seeing the case on the news although it was fifteen years ago. I remember the newspapers and TV being full of it at the time in Newcastle.'

I rack my brain, but without knowing what it's about, I shake my head. 'What was the story?'

'Well, a whole family were in a house fire. The wife, sister and brother died and only the husband, Peter Davies, and one son, Michael Davies managed to get out and survive.'

I feel a thud of excitement in my chest. I reckon I would have been seventeen at the time and to be honest reading newspapers and watching news on TV in the young offenders' institution hadn't been a regular pastime. I shake aside the sad memories and concentrate upon the here and now.

'No, I can't remember that story at all.'

Geoff smiles. 'Not to worry, there'll be lots of old newspaper reports to sift through.'

My mind races. 'So, what's happened now to put a different slant on the case?'

'Well,' Geoff says. 'Peter Davies, the father has just died but before he passed over, he told his son that he actually started the fire.'

'You've got to be kidding!' I shout.

Geoff laughs. 'I know, it's amazing how things happen, isn't it? I'm glad to see you're enjoying the work and throwing yourself in at the deep end,' he says. 'And I have to say, I'm impressed with you so far, Clive, so let's see what you make of this case.'

I nod and grin. 'I'd love to. I didn't realise that confessing things when you're dying was such a common thing - have you had many of these cases?'

Geoff nods. 'Well, I seem to have had a few together for some reason. Before these three cases, I hadn't been consulted with a deathbed confession for years. And, of course, there could be more, but these are the only ones I hear about when I'm asked to help,' he says rubbing his hands together. 'The last case in 2019 was a twin mix up.'

I gasp and lean forwards. 'A mix up? But how can that happen?'

'Well, apparently, a guy who thought he was, Nigel Smith, was actually Neil Smith. His twin sadly died in a cot death at home and when his father registered the death, he mixed the twins up. When his mother told him before she died it had a terrible effect on him and he's going through the rigmarole of changing his name back to Neil on the deed poll. Apart from missing his twin, he'd felt all his life that something was amiss and suffered an identity crisis.'

I shake my head and whistle between my teeth. 'That would knock you for six. I wonder why the mother, who obviously knew Nigel from Neil, didn't say anything about the mistake in the registry office?'

Geoff sighs. 'Apparently, his father had been handy with his fists, and she'd been scared of him.'

I tut in disgust and wander back to my desk while Geoff gets ready to leave for Leeds. He calls, 'See you.' and rushes out of the door.

I take a deep breath and dial Rose's number. I brace myself for more tears. She answers on the third ring.

'Hi, Rose, how are you?'

I figure, it's always best to start polite conversation with an enquiry as to someone's general health. However, in this case it sounds flippant because Rose must be feeling absolutely devasted.

'Hi, there, Clive. I'm okay, thanks.'

I can tell just by this sentence and the sound of her voice that she's so much better and breathe a sigh of relief.

'My dad turned up on the doorstep yesterday from Spain,' she says. 'He told me that although he couldn't face the funeral his conscience got the better of him, and well, here he is!'

My insides swell and I relax my shoulders knowing the conversation is going to be much easier. Also, my conscience won't prick if I leave her in floods of tears again because she won't be on her own. 'Well, that's great – isn't it?'

'Oooh, yeah, it's good to have him here. Dad has been telling me about things I didn't know, and we've talked through everything which has helped to settle my mind about Jake.'

I raise my eyebrow desperate to know myself. 'He has?' I ask. 'So, could you tell me now, Rose?'

I can almost hear her sweet smile. 'Yes, of course, Dad has gone up to town for a newspaper,' she says. 'Apparently, in all of the hullabaloo at the riverside that day, he'd had his suspicions about Jake and never quite believed Daisy had simply drowned. It had been the look on Jake's face when he'd got there which spooked him. Dad reckoned if a child was drowning and you were trying to rescue them, you'd look panic-stricken and shocked. But Jake didn't. He'd had a look of smug satisfaction on his face and Dad says his blood had ran cold.'

I gasp knowing my earlier thoughts had been proven right. Her father had known. To be so disturbed as to drown a little girl, young Jake must have shown other signs of poor mental health growing up. This type of vengeance wouldn't have occurred overnight, and her father had probably seen his warped mind materialise enough to rouse his suspicions.

'I'm so sorry to hear that, Rose,' I mutter, not knowing what more I can say to ease this awful discovery.

I need to put the conversation onto a more professional basis now. 'So, Geoff will have to report this confession to the police and coroner and then it'll be up to them what happens next.'

Rose sighs but sounds calm and contained. 'Yes, that's understandable. Dad has already said he's going to talk to them. So, going forward I won't need your services any longer because Dad will sort out everything that needs to be done,' she says. 'But thanks for your help when you came to the cottage. I was in such a state and really appreciate your kindness, Clive.'

I hang up thinking it's amazing the difference family support makes to a person. I can tell Rose has had a happy reunion with her father and hopefully he'll help her work through the grief over Jake. It's so very sad, I think recording our conversation and closing down the brown folder.

It's a pity I couldn't find some type of closure with my own father, however, I don't know if he's dead or alive now. Hopefully, it's the former, I grimace and run my hand through my hair.

Barbie reckons counselling would help because long term hatred isn't good for the soul. However, I wouldn't spend a penny of my money towards anything he did to me – it's too grotesque to even remember. My mother had died of alcoholic poisoning when I was in the institution, and I never shed a tear. When I was taken from the house my father was still there in his drugged stupor. And later, I'd had a certain gratification in knowing he would have missed the benefit they used to call family allowance. So, I think, in a warped way, at least my leaving affected him with less cash in his pocket. I shake my head in an effort to disperse the awful thoughts.

Picking up the email from Geoff, I begin to read. I learn that Peter Davies was forty-five years old when he died two months ago from cancer. His son, Michael is twenty-five. According to Sherrie, Peter had grasped Michael's hand before he took his last breaths and said these chilling words, 'The fire wasn't an accident - I started it.'

Throwing myself into as much preliminary research I can find, I read records, and 2007 death certificates of Michael's mother and siblings which sparks my curiosity. There are numerous court-case posts from local newspapers, mainly, The Evening Chronicle in Newcastle.

I neatly put everything I've printed into a new brown folder and then write, Michael Davies, on the front with a plan of action. My first task is to talk with Sherrie and Michael, so I answer the email hoping for a meeting with them on Monday. Within minutes an email pings back confirming two o'clock at their flat in Harrogate.

Chapter Ten

There's a light tap on the door, and I swing around in my chair. I do hope it's not Margaret again and hurry to open the door. The man who steps inside the office must be at least six foot three and very thin. He only has a smattering of hair left around the sides of his head and is wearing gold-rimmed glasses.

He holds out his hand. 'Good afternoon, I'm Neil Smith and had thought Geoff would be here,' he says. 'And you are?'

I introduce myself remembering the case of mixed up twins. Hoping to put this man at ease, I say, 'Geoff has left the office for the day, but I know all about your case so please take a seat and make yourself comfortable.'

'Ah, that's a shame,' he says, walking into the office. 'As I'm down here in York for the day, I figured I would pop in to leave Geoff a cheque for his services.'

I reckon he looks around mid-forties and is wearing jeans and a white T-shirt with a multi-coloured striped waistcoat. I think in the seventies they were called a tank top. I offer him a coffee, but he refuses.

He takes a seat, and says, 'When I made my first contact it was to ask if I needed to inform anyone at the town hall in Corbridge about the confusion over our names. And I'd also asked Geoff if burying the wrong son was a crime and whether the police should be informed?'

I reassure him this wouldn't be classed as a crime because both his parents and Nigel were now dead. And no one can be prosecuted once the perpetrator has died.

He nods and sighs heavily. 'Thank you,' he mumbles. 'Also, I wanted to let Geoff know that my name has now been officially changed by deed poll – it's taken a while because of the pandemic backlog.'

Conversationally, I say, 'That's good, although it seems that companies are using this as an excuse at the moment, but I suppose the backlog could be genuine.'

Neil makes a steeple with his fingers on the desk and nods. 'Maybe, but if government departments are as busy as we've been with less staff, then maybe the excuse is valid.'

I can't remember if Geoff told me what Neil did for a living but I'm soon to find out when he tells me about his job.

'I've worked all my life in Newcastle University science laboratory and suppose people would call me a science boffin although I hate the terminology,' he says. 'And that's why I hadn't wanted to use a PI in Newcastle just in case I was recognised.'

I smile knowing this guy obviously has a good reputation in the world of science. 'Well, that's more than understandable, do you live in Newcastle?'

'I do now,' he says. 'When Mother died, I sold our big house in Corbridge for an outrageous amount of money and bought a new-build flat down on Newcastle Quayside.'

He taps his fingers together now but doesn't smile. In fact, I haven't seen him smile once since he entered the room. His face remains serious although he does sit further back in the chair, so I hope he's relaxing.

I try again to bring him into friendly conversation. 'It must have been a big shock when you found out what had happened?'

'Yes, of course, it was. My mother, Christine Robinson died aged sixty five from cervical cancer and before she died, she told me I wasn't Nigel, but Neil Robinson,' he says sardonically. 'So yes, you could say that.'

I rest back and swing my computer chair a little from side to side wondering how this seemingly strait-laced man had reacted. 'And did she tell you how this had happened?'

His small beady eyes lose their sharpness and soften. 'She'd said that at eight months my brother and I were so identical my father couldn't tell us apart although she always could. And when she'd found Nigel dead in his cot, father had made the mistake when registering my twin's death. He'd simply mixed us up,' he says, looking over my shoulder towards the window.

There's almost a wistful expression now on his face when he continues, 'Mother had been too scared of him to say he'd made a mistake, and he was wrong. So, she pretended I was Nigel to keep the peace,' he says. 'She also told me it hadn't really mattered because she loved me so much anyway.'

'But it did matter to you?'

Neil gets up and begins to stride around the small room. 'Of course, it did! After living all my life as one brother, I suddenly found out I wasn't who I'd thought I was. I was really Neil, first born by three minutes.'

He stops by my chair and looks down at my name plate on the desk. Raising an eyebrow, and with an authoritative air to his voice, he says, 'I don't know if you're aware of this, Clive, but identical twins share a particularly intense bond. They are the result of one fertilized egg splitting into two, giving them identical DNA.'

'I didn't know that,' I say, although I did. 'But please continue.'

'Well, apart from missing my twin I'd felt all my life that something was amiss,' he says. 'I've often wondered if we would have been like other twins who finish each other's sentences and have the special connection beyond that of ordinary siblings.'

I nod and smile as he paces. 'And your father?'

'Father died ten years ago in a road traffic accident which was caused by a crazed motorcyclist, and we mourned him for years,' he says. 'Had I known he'd been such a bully to my mother that wouldn't have happened!'

Jeez, I think. All of this hurt and upset because of a man making one mistake in the registry office. It had turned out to be hugely significant to the remaining twin. The mistake had caused years of turmoil for the mother, and now terrible anguish for Neil to live with for the rest of his life. The poor guy is all alone in the world and has probably buried himself in his laboratory amongst science where feelings don't come into his daily timetable.

It's almost as though he can read my mind when he says, 'I never married and was a bit of a loner with no friends because there was only ever me and my mother up until her death. After this happened, I would look in the mirror feeling lost and asking the question, who am I? I began to hate her for lying and being so weak that she put her fear of my father before my wellbeing.'

I sigh. I feel like telling him about my miserable childhood which may help to put his existence into some type of perspective, but I don't. All I say is, 'It can't have been easy for her though.'

He stops pacing and sits back down in the chair. 'I realise that now after having counselling sessions in the university. The counsellor told me I was suffering from a major identity crisis and there was only ever employment in my work-life balance. I'm what's known as a lone twin, and apparently there are thousands of twin-less twins around the world who unite through organizations and online groups to share support. She gave me these details, advice and reassurance which helped beyond measure.'

'Oh, that's so good,' I say.

There's a shy expression on his face now when he says, 'I took two months off work and went on a world cruise. I joined in groups on the ship and met some really nice people especially a lady called Pauline who was starting again after a messy divorce. We found a lot in common with each other and are now courting.'

He smiles for the first time which seems to change all the contours of his face. His small eyes have a sunny twinkle in them.

'In fact, she's waiting for me in the park, so I need to get going.'

I grin, walk with him to the door and shake his hand. Locking the cheque safely away in my desk drawer I think about the old-fashioned term, courting. It's something that would have been used years ago but decide it suits this science boffin perfectly. Whistling a tuneless jingle, I head off home loving a happy ending.

Chapter Eleven

Barbie had messaged earlier to say that she'd asked Simon and June to dinner which was a nice surprise. I wander up through the city towards our home on Victor Street which is in a quiet secluded area. The small terrace of houses has only a pedestrian access through an old arch way at one end.

I've loved living here since I moved in with my ex-wife. It's close enough to walk into the city for work and shopping, but far enough to be away from the hustle and bustle. The street is short with less houses compared to others in the vicinity. All the houses, including ours, have attractive and enclosed fore-courted gardens leading through gates to the front entrance doors. There are four houses further down the street which have new windows but mostly, like ours, they are old.

On the way, I chat to a couple of our neighbours and then stand at our red front door deciding the grass needs cutting. I'm not a keen gardener and see it is as a necessary chore like cleaning the windows. However, Barbie enjoys tending the garden more than I do, so we have a pact. I cut the grass back and front, she weeds, plants flowers, and keeps the old garden shed tidy.

I wander through the lounge and wonder why the table isn't set for our meal. The back door is open, and I can hear Barbie clattering in the garden. Heading outside, I gasp in surprise. It's not a big garden but substantial in relation to the size of the terraced house. We have two fold-up picnic tables in the shed which she has put together and covered with a white table cloth. The table is set with our best crockery and cutlery, wine glasses, tumblers and two big water jugs. She has also trailed fairy lights from the two big trees on either side of the central grass.

'Hey,' I call and hurry to her. 'This looks brilliant!'

Barbie is dressed in a pink skirt and T-Shirt. I can tell she's caught the sun from being outdoors all day and I kiss the tip of her nose.

She giggles. 'Well, it's such a lovely summer evening I thought we could eat outside,' she says, and hugs me. 'They're coming in half an hour, so shower and change while I finish up here.'

I do as she bids and pull on a pair of knee-length denim shorts and blue vest. While I'm dressing, I look down at her from the bedroom window. I take a second to stand still and watch her setting out a long plate with a side of poached salmon, two bowls of salad and what looks like my favourite Jersey Royal potatoes. She's amazing and I still can't believe my luck in finding her that day in The Shambles.

It had been during the pandemic, and I was at home furloughed from the travel agency. I'd been shopping and was carrying my food in a plastic bag which suddenly split. Barbie was walking past but stopped to hurry after my wayward tins of beans in the gutter. She returned them to me laughing. And that was it. We clicked. We stood looking at each other and corny as it seemed, I had known in seconds that she was special. I reckoned this happenchance meeting had occurred for a reason. We were meant to be together.

I hear voices downstairs and hurry to greet Simon and June. Barbie is hugging June when I reach the bottom of the stairs, and I shake Simon's hand. I'm gobsmacked to see that Simon has ditched his sweater and is wearing a green dress shirt, although the corduroys are still in place. It pleases me to think he's made such a monumental effort to come to our home. We lead them both through the kitchen and outside into the garden.

Simon grins and whispers behind me at the doorway. 'I see what you mean about the red kitchen!'

'Yeah, I told you it was horrendous, but don't mention it to Barbie or she'll have me looking at kitchen brochures.'

He chortles and pulls at the collar of his shirt. I can see he's uncomfortable and while June exclaims at the lovely dining prospect, I place Simon at the head of the table under the willow tree for shade.

'You'll be a little cooler here,' I say, and he nods his thanks.

June is petite like Barbie but very thin. Not that I'm saying my Barbie is overweight because she isn't – she's just cuddly in all of the right places. I love her just the way she is, simply perfect.

Wearing a long orange skirt and gypsy top, I notice June's very thin clavicles and neck. She has amazing clear supple skin, and I figure she takes advantage of the beauty treatments on offer where she works in the Turkish Baths. I open wine and pour it out for the others but fill a tumbler of sparkling water for myself as we settle together comfortably around the table.

Barbie says, 'And, we don't want you two guys talking about writing all night – do we June?'

June smiles and I see her small grey eyes shining. 'Oh, I don't mind if it makes them happy,' she says, waving nonchalantly. 'We can talk about other things, Barbara.'

I smile and pile my plate with salmon, salad, and potatoes. Realising Barbie has forgotten the mayonnaise, I head back to the kitchen and as I get it out of the fridge my mobile tinkles with an email.

I know I shouldn't because we have guests, but I open the email while heading back into the garden. It's from a publisher who I'd contacted about my latest book. I read, 'Thank you for your novel submission, Clive. We may be interested in working with you on your next novel. And, as the Crime Writers' Festival is coming up soon in Harrogate, we'd like to meet with you there - if this is convenient?'

My whole insides soar. I rattle the jar of mayonnaise onto the table and whoop so loudly that Barbie drops her fork.

'OMG!' I shout. 'I'm sorry, Barbie, I know you said no writing talk, but I can't believe this!'

Simon leans over to me and takes my phone to read the email. 'Jeez, Clive, that's great news! If they're coming up to The Old Swan for the festival, it'll be great to meet them in person rather by email.'

My stomach is doing somersaults and my hand trembles as I pick up the tumbler. I gulp down mouthfuls of water and then explain to Barbie and June my good news from the submissions editor.

I look at Simon and grin. 'Oh, I do hope so. To have a publisher would be my dream come true!'

I look up and see Barbie heading my way. She stands behind me and wraps her arms around my neck then kisses my temple. 'Well done, darling,' she whispers. 'I'm so very proud of you. And as this is a special announcement you can talk about it all night long!'

June laughs along with Barbie and congratulates me too.

Simon leans over and claps me on the shoulder saying, 'It's well deserved, as you told me and this will give you even more push to write the new novel, not that you needed any, but it's always good to have a goal to aim for.'

I laugh out loud and relax my shoulders. My stomach settles and is replaced with pangs of hunger. I tuck into the food with gusto. Simon holds up his wine glass and the women join him when he wishes me all the very best of luck.

While the women discuss fashions, Simon and I plan our three day visit to the festival. 'I'll email them back in the morning and suggest a lunch meeting, although it depends how many days they'll be in Harrogate and what time they have available.'

As the sun goes down behind the shed, we clear the table and head inside to sit in comfort while Barbie makes coffee. Simon and I sink into the sofa and having exhausted the plans for the festival, I tell him about Geoff at work.

Simon nods at intervals but doesn't comment until I've finished. I decide that listening is one of his best virtues.

'It's just that I can't seem to get Geoff off my mind,' I say. 'And if I'm to continue working with him, I need to know who this man is? I'm loving the actual work but it's the suspicion surrounding Geoff that's bugging me.'

'Well,' Simon says, furrowing his thick eyebrows. 'I have to say, it does sound suspicious, but be careful – you don't want to end up in the middle of a tricky divorce case. That is, if he is guilty of what his wife claims.'

I nod and rub my jaw. 'I know, but I reckon the only way to gather more information about Geoff and his shenanigans is to follow him,' I say. 'That way, I'll get a handle on his day to day life when he's not working or in the office. It might give me an idea of his home life with Margaret.'

Simon nods and yawns. He looks at June and she smiles. I see they have the same connection as a couple who've been together a long time, which Barbie and I have. Without June speaking, I know they're getting ready to leave.

They thank Barbie once more for the delicious food and make their way to the front door.

Barbie hugs June, and says, 'Thanks for offering to put Clive up at your house for the three day festival next week.'

'Aww, it's not a problem, in fact it'll be great to have a house guest,' June says. 'And, Barbara you can join him if you want to – we've plenty of room?'

Barbie shakes her head. 'Thanks, June but I'm going up to Durham to stay with my mam for the weekend. I haven't seen the family for a few weeks, and it'll be a good chance to catch up with everything I've missed.'

Locking the front door, I offer to clear up and Barbie heads upstairs to bed. My mind is still buzzing at the offer to meet a publisher and I know sleep won't come easy tonight.

Chapter Twelve

After tossing and turning until late, I wake early the next morning and leave Barbie asleep. I decide to follow Geoff and see what I can discover. Pulling on my jeans, I decide it'll be a good way to test my surveillance skills.

Within thirty minutes, I'm wandering over Skeldergate Bridge with the sun already shining. It's going to be a lovely day, I reckon and tingle with excitement every time I think of next weekend's writing festival.

In my strange, irrational way, which I figure comes from a miserable childhood, I decide it's best not to get too excited and hopeful about the outcome. If they turn me down, I'll be devastated and crushed from a giddy height. However, if I stay calm and keep a slightly pessimistic view on the meeting, then I won't have as far to fall. But who am I kidding, I sigh, whichever way it turns, I'll be shattered if they don't take me onto their authors' list.

The publisher's website is amazing with a long list of established authors and fantastic books. Some of which I've read and am well impressed. When I think of my own work, I'm never sure if it hits this high standard, but Barbie reckons it does, and my doubts are because I had the confidence knocked out of me when I was little.

When she was a child, Mr and Mrs Webster praised and congratulated Barbie pushing her on to be bigger and better in everything she did at school and then university. I sigh with longing to have had this start in life. It would have made me a more confident person.

However, Mrs Webster had once said, 'On the other side of the coin, any success you've had since leaving the institution has been all the more appreciated because you had to work harder and drag yourself up by your own wit and ingenuity.'

I wonder if this struggle is apparent in my writing and imagination in scenes, plots, and characters? I know deep down that my past will always be part of my psychological persona and will never leave me.

I pause half way across the bridge and lean over the old stone sides looking out to Tower Place which is where Geoff lives. There are six red dingy-boats roped together in front of the wide riverside path. A man with a high-viz jacket is tending to them and I smile knowing he's got a nice job in the summer weather.

Beyond the path, are the Edwardian houses on Friar's Place which is where our friend, Rodger lives. I suddenly wonder if he knows Margaret and Geoff? If it's true that Margaret has lived there all her life, there's a good chance he'll be able to give me some information about them. Margaret or Geoff have never been at our neighbourhood watch meetings before which are held in Rodger's house, but he might well know them simply as neighbours.

I continue over the bridge, buy a coffee and then stand across the road from the opening to Tower Place. The situation is ideal because there's only one way in, which is down an alleyway. I sip the hot coffee out of a carton. I'm not exactly sure what I'll find, probably nothing I decide, but lift my shoulders thinking it's the start of the trail.

I know Geoff's house number so I can loiter around in my dark jeans and blue sweater. I remember the on-line guidelines for conducting surveillance I'd read at the caravan park when trailing the German suspect.

The most important thing is to wear dark clothes, or clothes that don't stand out in a throng of people. It's best to try and blend into the landscape as it were.

When I see the alleyway is empty, I cross the road and read a white sign on the end house. No Through Way. Tower Place. Leading To Back South Esplanade.

The alleyway is as pristine as any you'd like to see and use. Obviously, an upmarket alley, if there is such a thing. There's no dried urine smell hanging around, nor loose or bagged rubbish. It's spotlessly clean with hanging baskets of flowers on one side of the wall.

Looking around, I conclude there's nothing here to help. There's no giant sign saying, this way to find out about Geoff and his illicit affair with Jemma. Smiling, I imagine the thought of Jemma wearing a kilt and singing, "Bonnie Banks of Loch Lomond" to prove that yes, she was here, and yes, she was waiting for Geoff. I chortle. This would be concrete proof he was having an affair and telling lies to Margaret.

If only life was that easy, I muse and drink the hot coffee. There's no sign of Geoff, but I don't want to walk around in front of his big bay windows in case he sees me. I head down the next street and see his car parked up. I recognise the colour and make from being outside the office.

As I settle myself for a long wait, I drain the coffee and toss the carton into a bin. Suddenly, I see the back of Geoff coming out of the door. I recognise his brown suede jacket and beige trousers. He throws an expensive looking leather bag of golf clubs into his car boot, jumps in, and drives off.

I frown. Failed at the first hurdle, I think and know I would need Barbie's car to follow him. However, as if by a miracle, Rodger's partner, Paul turns onto the street. I wave when he approaches, and we stop to chat.

'Hey, there,' I say shaking his hand. 'I couldn't have seen you at a better time.'

'Oh, that sounds ominous,' he says laughing.

Paul is a lawyer and works further down in the city. He's a good-looking guy, even more so in his black suit. I ask, 'How come you're working on a Saturday?'

'Ah, we're really busy at the moment for some reason,' he says. 'How's you and Barbara?'

'We're good thanks, but like you busy, so we haven't been to a neighbourhood watch meeting for a while.'

Paul nods. 'To be honest, Rodger hasn't held any for a few months because he's up to his eyes with an art exhibition that's making him sweat!'

Thinking of Rodger, I smile with fondness at his flamboyant dress and lifestyle. He is definitely one of the kindest men I've ever met. I say this, not because he gave me a beautiful painting, but also for how much he does in the community.

I explain briefly about working with Geoff Smithson and ask if they know him and Margaret. And, what type of people they are.

Paul nods. 'Yes, of course, we know where they live, but I've never actually been in their company. I can't think Rodger has either. They tend to keep themselves to themselves, as it were,' he says. 'I could be wrong, but I think Rodger has sold paintings to Margaret's father in the past who started the interior design business she runs now.'

I smile my thanks and can see Paul is itching to get off. 'Look, thanks for that,' I say. 'I won't keep you any longer form work.'

'No Worries,' Paul says, and turns to leave. 'I'll check with Rodger later and if there's any juicy gossip to report I'll get him to ring you.'

I turn in the opposite direction as we call goodbye and walk back across Skeldergate Bridge feeling slightly dejected and disappointed. So, I transgress, out of my first surveillance on Geoff, I've achieved absolutely zilch. The man has simply gone off to play golf on a weekend which isn't an irregular activity. In fact, it's what many men do to relax.

I grunt, it's only idiots like me who come up with ridiculous things to do on a Saturday morning. However, I determine not to give up and know I'll figure out another way to see what Geoff does while he's at home. Thinking of Barbie, I wonder if she's still in bed and would like to show me just how proud she really is, and grin.

Chapter Thirteen

I'm on the train to Harrogate the next afternoon knowing with a thirty minute journey, I'll be there in good time. Depending upon how long it takes to see Michael and Sherrie, I plan to go to Simon's house afterwards so we can go along to the writing group together. Cynthia has called an extra group meeting to discuss the author interview spot we need to organise.

Alighting from the train, I head outside through the main doors into a sky full of thick cloud. The sun has left us today, although it's still warm. I hope it's not going to rain because I haven't brought a jacket.

The first thing I see is a gigantic pink high-heeled shoe which is filled with flowers in the square of the new shopping centre. I say, newish because the shopping centre was built in 1992 whereas the other designer shops in town are further down in older buildings.

The plaque underneath the shoe tells me it's part of The Floral Summer of Celebration.

Whipping out my mobile, I send Barbie a photo with a message, 'Is this shoe big enough for you?' I end the text with a smiley emoji and two pink hearts.

I head down into town and see the usual queue outside the world-famous Betty's tearooms. People stand in line outside from early in the morning until it closes to taste the amazing cakes and pastries. The plaque outside tells me, it is an iconic family business founded in 1919 with Swiss-Yorkshire heritage, although the identity of Betty remains a mystery. Alongside the café is a shop where you can buy everything boxed to take home. Mrs Webster adores their Bakewell tarts, but as we have a Betty's in York too, Barbie often buys them for her.

Heading along to Victoria Avenue I pass the designer shops and high-class jewellers. I look in the largest shop window which is where I bought Barbie's engagement ring and grin. Maybe, we'll choose our wedding rings from here too.

I walk through the library car park appreciating the surrounding old Yorkshire stone-built houses and offices. Most are three storeys high, where each of the floors are rented by small businesses.

Hmm, I think, it's different to the new build office Geoff rents in York and wonder if the rates are higher here. I'd found Raglan Street on the map before leaving home so have a good idea where I'm going which is opposite to the library.

This street of terraced houses looks well-kept and it's obvious people in Harrogate take pride in their homes. Simon's favourite saying is, 'We are proud to be from Yorkshire and it shows.'

Since the start of the pandemic when everyone was restricted to travel, and holidays seemed a thing of the past, home renovations increased dramatically. Builders and manufacturers were inundated with demand. I remember Barbie searching for days to buy paint and a small picket fence for our back garden. And then later, finding someone to install the fence took even longer. I have to admit that I'm pretty useless at DIY and don't even possess a drill. Sad but true.

I groan looking at these gardens to see nicely cut grassy areas. I still haven't cut our grass at home and know Barbie will be within her rights to ride my case. I count the numbers of houses while I walk along the street until I come to the end semi-detached and can see there's three buttons on an intercom buzzer system. I hop up the stone steps and press number one, with Davies written next to the button.

A young female voice answers and says, 'Come in, Clive.'

***

I open the big black door and step into a huge hallway. The floor is laid with original ceramic geometric tiles, and I whistle through my teeth in awe. The height of the ceiling and coving is amazing and a newer white door with a black number 1 opens on my left.

I spin around and see a blonde woman I figure must be Sherrie.

'Hey there,' I say, and give her what I hope is a winning smile. Barbie often says this smile makes me look like a grinning idiot, but I persevere.

Sherrie Williams is what I'd call a brassy blonde. She's wearing a short, and I mean, short mini skirt with skinny legs tucked into knee-high brown boots.

'Come on through,' she says, stepping aside.

When I pass by her, I smell a sweet cloying perfume which Barbie reckons is a sign of cheap imitation. Sherrie has a long snake tattoo down the side of her neck. I'm not a lover of tattoos although they seem to be getting more and more popular nowadays. On this young girl, it gives a hard line look. But maybe, I muse, this is what she's trying to achieve.

Stepping into the hall, I look around at the clean painted walls and polished wood floor leading into the big open plan lounge. I follow her through unable to take my eyes off her girlish wiggle as she walks.

The lounge is an airy room with a massive bay window where light floods into every corner. 'What a beautiful room,' I say, looking around.

Sherrie gestures to the brown sofa and I take a seat noticing what a good match the colour is with the wood flooring.

She smiles coyly and nods. 'Thank you, we love it, and our landlord is a great guy,' she says. 'We often hear bad reports on TV about rogue property owners who let out their places in bad repair, but we've been lucky to find this one.'

I admire the two standard lamps with trendy shades, luxurious cream drapes at the window and wonder if Sherrie has put this together or if it was part-furnished. She takes a seat in the adjoining armchair and seems to sink into it whilst crossing her little legs.

I agree with her comment and study her face. Her long yellow hair is obviously coloured out of a bottle and her face is heavily made-up with long eyelashes caked in thick mascara on baby-blue eyes. I can't help wondering what she'd look like without the brassiness because somehow it doesn't work with her genteel spoken voice. This harsh look would suit a gobby, uneducated accent which she doesn't have.

'I can see you're looking around for Michael,' she says. 'He's in bed because he worked an extra night shift, but he'll be up shortly.'

I nod. 'It can't be easy working as a hospital porter at the moment with everything that's happened in the NHS?'

Sherrie smiles. 'You're right there, it's been a hard couple of years because we both work at York Hospital,' she says. 'I'm an assistant in pharmacy and if we're on the same shift I drive us there, but if not, Michael takes the train especially for night shift.'

She offers to make tea and hurries through into the kitchen at the back of the open plan area. I watch her movements around the kitchen, switching on the kettle, and dipping down into the fridge for milk.

Suddenly, a man pops his head around the lounge door. 'Hi, you must be Clive, sorry I wasn't here when you arrived.'

I stand up to shake his hand. 'Er, that's not a problem. If I'd been on night shift, I would still be sound asleep.'

Michael is wearing a green dressing gown over pyjama bottoms and slopes into the lounge. He plonks down into the chair which Sherrie has vacated. He's medium height and build, and looks about the same age as Sherrie, although I know from the newspaper articles, he's twenty five.

'Nice to meet you, Michael,' I say, and perch back down on the edge of the sofa. I take the mug of tea from Sherrie and watch her place Michael's cup on the coffee table next to him. I can tell this is his chair which is mostly turned towards the TV.

Even though I've read all the newspaper articles about the fire I still want to hear Michael's account of exactly what happened that night. As the saying goes, never believe what you read in the papers, and know his version will be the correct one to base the investigation upon. If Michael does want to take his step mother to court and claim inheritance monies, we'll need all the information gathered correctly for the case.

'So, Michael, I'm here to get all of the fundamental details then if we have any questions or more information that we need, I'll refer back to Mr Smithson for guidance and answers.'

He turns to look at Sherrie and she smiles at him. She explains to Michael. 'Clive means the basics, Michael.'

Michael is what Mrs Webster would call a pretty boy, with cropped, blonde curly hair and a goatee beard. He fastens the dressing gown tighter around his middle and nods at me in understanding. I can tell it was the word, fundamental, which had confused him and decide to use a more communal language. Sherrie's email said Michael suffered from slight learning difficulties.

He smiles at me for the first time with small white teeth. I feel transfixed at what this smile does to his face – he's certainly a great looking young guy. I decide to hit the ground running and ask, 'So, if it's not too painful for you, Michael, can you tell me about the night of the fire?'

I pull a small flip notebook and pen from the back pocket of my jeans. I look at them both and raise my eyebrow to gain consent for taking notes. Sherrie nods and I begin to scribble.

Michael shuffles on the chair. I notice how long his fingers are when he twirls them on a thick gold chain around his neck. He begins, 'Well, the fire started at the front door and when I did manage to run through the lounge and out of the back door, I saw Dad standing in the garden. But Mam wasn't with him.'

Michael takes a deep breath. His light eyebrows furrow and his small grey eyes cloud over.

'Take your time,' I say, and give him an encouraging smile to continue. 'You're doing great.'

He nods. 'Then after a few seconds the whole downstairs seemed to be ablaze. My brother, sister, and Mam were upstairs in their beds, but I'd fallen asleep on the sofa and Dad had left me there before going up to bed himself. There were bright-orange, climbing flames and I remember staring at them as if I was in some type of trance. I'd been startled at a horrible loud noise – it was like a howling wolf which at the time I couldn't understand. But later a firefighter told me it was the noise flames make when gathering speed,' he says, and covers his ears with his hands.

I sigh. It's as though he can still hear the noises and my heart squeezes for him. I've never even see a big fire ablaze so wouldn't know what or how it felt to be in amongst the flames and smoke. Obviously, Michael is reliving it all now, and I say, 'Do you want to stop?'

He shakes his head and fixes a look of determination on his pretty face. 'Nooo, I'll keep going,' he says, and frowns. 'So, within what seemed like minutes it was an inferno and quickly got out of control. Dad stood still staring at the house – his face was white. My grannie told me later it's what happens to a person when they're in shock. I…I remember there was no reaction from him. His eyes were dead. There was no tears or sound from him at all. He just stood and watched.'

I nod and turn to Sherrie who takes Michael's hand and squeezes it tight. 'Get it all out, Michael, and then it'll be over,' she says.

I'm scribbling as fast as I can and curse myself for not bringing a recorder or learning how to record on my mobile. Note to myself, get this sorted asap.

His gentle face scowls now. 'Ha! Now I know why he wasn't surprised because he knew it was going to happen,' he snarls looking down at his hands. 'Anyway, dogs in the street were barking and pandemonium had broken out. Our Indian neighbours tried to get inside, but they were beaten back by the flames and smoke. The firefighters eventually put out the blaze and found Mam and my brother dead in their beds, b…but they managed to get my sister out alive, although she died later in hospital. Me and dad were taken to a hotel in Newcastle near the RVI hospital as my sister fought for her life in ITU, or at least that's what he told me.'

Michael's face is pale now and I see terror widen his eyes at the memories. He takes another deep breath and wrings his hands together to stop them from shaking. Pulling constantly on the fingers on his right hand, he cracks his knuckles. Sherrie leans over, and puts both her hands on top of his, murmuring platitudes.

I look at him and in a soothing voice, I say, 'Hey, it's going to be okay – we can sort this out.'

Michael catches a sob in the back of his throat. He stutters, 'T…The police immediately began to look for clues to discover how the fire had started and found a petrol lawnmower in the hall which had broken years ago but was empty. Afterwards, they said accelerant had been poured through the letterbox on the front door. Whoever had done it had used far too much petrol and hadn't known the quantity to make a small fire. For months afterwards, Dad was questioned by the police, but there was nothing to charge him with, other than not trying to rescue his family alongside the neighbours. Dad sold our story to a local newspaper and said he got mega bucks for it, a…and within two months of Mam dying in the fire, he had another partner!'

I sit back on the sofa and shake my head in disbelief. This man, Peter Davies, must have been a real piece of work, I reckon and tut loudly. How could he do this to his own family? And if that wasn't bad enough, to sell his story was downright despicable. I watch Michael take deep breaths in and out slowly and see a little colour coming back into his face.

Michael asks, 'So, can you find out how much dad got for our story in the newspaper?'

I jot this down in my notebook. 'Well, I'll certainly see what I can do,' I say. 'And was this when you moved down here to Harrogate?'

He nods. 'I moved to get away from Dad because I was sick of him scrounging the money I'd worked for at the General Hospital in Newcastle. I got a transfer to York and then moved in here with Sherrie.'

I notice the way Sherrie looks at him with eyes full of love and care. She picks up the story now. 'Last month we got a call from Newcastle and went to see his dad because he was dying. We sat at his bedside with his new wife,' she says. 'Michael never liked her because she was as money grabbing as he was.'

I nod and mutter, 'That's understandable.'

Sherrie asks, 'Is this what's called theft through fraud?'

I'm not sure and write this down in my notebook knowing I can ask Geoff.

Michael looks back to his normal self now and leans towards me. 'Can you find out if my dad left any money, like life insurance? I'd hate the bitch to get it all because if anyone should have the money, it's me! It would be pay back for all the times Dad scrounged my wages.'

I reassure them that I'll look into their questions and be back in touch when I have the answers from consulting with my boss. Sherrie walks back into the hall with me as I leave.

'Thanks for coming here, Clive,' she says. 'It would have been more difficult for Michael to come to the office in York. He would have felt intimated by it all, and no one likes getting upset in strange places. It's easier being at home.'

I smile. 'That's not a problem, I can always come out to you both here.'

She closes the door with a gentle click, and I reckon Michael is a lucky guy to have the love and support from this young woman.

Chapter Fourteen

Michael's mind buzzed now that Clive had left and hoped he'd answered all the questions correctly because he didn't want the PI to think he was thick and stupid. Sherrie had sprung the interview on him when he'd arrived home from his night shift - which wasn't good – he didn't like surprises and hadn't been prepared. Michael liked time to plan and think.

He headed into the shower and groaned knowing he should have dressed first instead of meeting him in his dressing gown. Michael stood under the stream of hot water. The next time Clive came, he'd make sure he wore his good clothes. It would show the PI, as his grannie had often said, 'Although you're not the sharpest tool in the box you do have good taste and style.'

Making a fresh cup of tea and slices of buttered toast, he recapped over the interview and everything they'd talked about. Michael remembered putting his hands over his ears, wringing his hands and cracking his knuckles, hoping to convince Clive about the trauma he'd suffered and have him believe his story. This was important because he wanted Clive on his side. Michael knew he'd have a better chance of getting money from the bitch his father married if Clive felt sorry for him.

Michael hadn't intended getting so wound up about the fire, but since his father's death, the confession was uppermost in his mind. When he'd told Clive about the sequence of events ten years ago it had brought the fire back to him in vivid colours. He'd remembered the sight and sounds of the flames along with the acrid taste of smoke in the back of his throat, and later the smell of smouldering ash.

He wandered into the bedroom and began to dress. He had bad-mouthed his dad to some degree which hadn't been his intention. But in his defence, he'd had to tell Clive about the aftermath, selling their story to the newspapers, and shacking up with someone else after only two months of his mam dying.

Plonking down on the stool at Sherrie's dressing table, Michael pushed his feet through a pair of socks and grimaced. It was hard not to be vindictive now he knew his father had actually started the fire. Although it was weeks since the revelation, he still couldn't believe Dad had actually done this.

Michael remembered sitting on the side of his deathbed. There'd been a strange smell in the room which reminded him of Parma Violet sweets. Sherrie seemed to think it was the smell of death, but he'd dismissed this as nonsense. At the time, Michael couldn't believe this big strapping man, who was his dad could possibly die. The bedside clock had ticked loudly in the silence of the bedroom reminding him of his parents' room in the old house before the fire.

Dad had beckoned him nearer and whispered those chilling five words, 'Michael, I started the fire!'

When he'd shaken his head in utter disbelief, Sherrie had put her hand on his shoulder and squeezed it tight. He'd thought he was hearing things, but his dad had simply nodded, breathed out loudly and passed.

A ball of acidy vomit had gathered in the back of his throat as he staggered from the bedroom propped up by Sherrie because his legs had given way. He couldn't remember getting downstairs and outside.

She'd bundled him onto the back seat of her car and drove them back to York.

He'd shivered and sobbed with a rug over him and later, Sherrie had said, 'You sounded like a wounded animal!'

Afterwards, he didn't mind admitting the confession had blown his mind apart. Sherrie had cuddled him for hours while he'd sobbed and eventually had taken a sedative from the GP to help him sleep.

Michael shrugged these thoughts aside now knowing the GP was right - it could take him months to come to terms with the shock. It had put his old memories into different sections in his mind and made him question whether they were real and had actually happened.

Pulling a sweater over his head, Michael smirked. He'd tried to paint a picture of happy families to Clive not wanting him to know about their true family set up. Just before the month of the fire, Michael had heard whispers in their kitchen.

Grannie had said, 'Your mam wants to leave you all.'

Michael struggled to understand this because Dad had been great. Yeah, he'd not had a job and knew the benefit system inside out but supported the family in other ways.

'Benefit City,' he often called the place. 'I've played the useless government and won – I've got every benefit going!'

Dad used to write and get paid for letters which were mainly complaints he sent to the newspapers. He'd been an expert at finding food vouchers for supermarkets and had always been lucky in the betting shop and winning *bingo in the club. Plus of course, he'd had the family allowance for all the kids.*

Grannie had also said, 'Your mam only ever wanted to have you, but your dad was so attractive she couldn't say no to him. In fact, that was her biggest problem because she couldn't say no to a lot of other men, too.'

Gossip about Mam began when Michael was at school and how she'd had affairs with other men in the area. It was whispered behind his back and his mates laughed, but only when his burly brother wasn't around. No one would ever tackle his brother, well not if they had a smattering of common sense, he had the reputation of being a thug at the age of fourteen.

Dad hated the Indian neighbours although Michael didn't. Mr Singh and his family were nice to him, and he'd gone to school with their son, Ali, and many of the other Indian children. Michael knew on the night of the fire they had been the people who tried to help them. The Indian men had ran towards the house, and tried to beat at the flames and smoke to get inside. He also remembered how the Indian women, dressed in their saris with dressing gowns on top, made them tea and snacks. He'd always thought them good people.

Michael heard Sherrie pottering about in the kitchen now and knew she wanted to go out for a walk, but he couldn't be bothered. However, he sneered knowing full well how to get around Sherrie and change her mind. She couldn't resist him.

Chapter Fifteen

Back outside on Raglan Street, I fill my lungs full of fresh air. It feels like a release from the tense atmosphere I've just been through in Michael and Sherrie's flat. I feel so sorry for Michael and what he's going through. And of course, what he went through as a fifteen year old in the fire.

It's often said, and rightly so because I'm a prime example, that childhood shapes a person's future. How you are raised plays a major part in your development well into teenage years and as young adults. Michael's childhood, like mine, was sadly lacking. This depravation made me determined to leave it in the past and turn my life around to be a better person. However, this is not always the case. Some young people don't or can't achieve a positive manner of thinking through no fault of their own.

I begin to walk down through the streets towards Kings Road where Simon lives. I'll be a little early for the writing group at five but know Simon will make coffee and we can have a catch up.

Kings Road runs along the side of the new convention centre where flats are intermingled with terraced houses. I stop outside his house and smile. I love the frontage of their home, it always makes me feel happy for some reason. The windows are big, wide and painted white. June has cleverly used white wood shutters inside on both front windows which are stunning. Above the two windows is a small attic window which is Simon's study.

The door is painted in racing green, and I remember Simon once saying, 'I'd always wanted a MGT car in this colour, but my salary never stretched that far, so I settled for the green colour on our front door.'

The long narrow garden leads up to the door, and I bite my lip, their grass is neatly cut too. I shrug, cutting our grass must be my first job tomorrow morning. I rap on the door using the chrome knocker and hear Simon like an elephant charging down the stairs.

'Hey, there,' he says, opening the door wide.

I smile and step inside. I see his baggy brown sweater is back in place. 'I'm early but figured you'd give a poor PI assistant a coffee.'

He laughs and leads me down the hall into their big kitchen diner at the back of the house. This too, is an amazing room with cream highly-glossed cabinets and counter tops. I look around in awe wondering if Barbie and I will ever own a house like this.

'I love this room,' I say wistfully, and perch myself on a black stool at the island in the centre.

'Me too,' he says. 'But in my opinion, it comes a very close second to your bright red kitchen.'

I nudge him playfully, and grin. 'Aww, give over,' I say. 'No, but seriously this house must be worth something now, Simon?'

He pours coffee into mugs from a percolator. There's no jar of instant here and I inhale the rich aroma. I sip the coffee and relax my shoulders feeling content in his friendly company.

'Probably,' he says. 'We bought it years ago when it wasn't quite the hip place to live in Harrogate. And it's all down to June who has great vision and style. She's renovated the place from top to bottom.'

We discuss my email from the publisher. 'So, I'm meeting with them on the Friday of the festival in the lounge of The Old Swan, and to say I'm excited is an understatement.'

Simon sits opposite cradling his mug of coffee. 'Oh, you'll certainly get taken on,' he says. 'I can't see them offering to meet if they weren't interested and unless you make a complete fool of yourself, you'll come away with a contract.'

'A fool of myself – me? Yeah, that's something I never do!'

I tell him about my escapade following Geoff on Saturday morning and we both laugh.

My stomach churns thinking of next week. 'But I've decided not to build myself up into a giddy state about the publishers, so I won't be crushed if they don't want me. I'm just going to play it cool.'

Simon shakes his head. 'Wrong thing to do there, mate, because you'll come across in a negative manner and that's the last thing they want to see. They'll expect you to be buzzing with ideas and enthusiasm. So, go for gold!'

He grabs his jacket. 'Are you okay walking back up to the library instead of using the car because I've promised June, I'll make an effort to exercise more.'

I agree and we leave the house. 'Good on you, Simon. Writing is a solitary occupation, and we spend hours sitting at our desks. Movement of any kind is a good thing.'

***

We are the first to arrive in the library basement and settle ourselves in the Victoria room at the table.

Simon is asking my opinion about where to leave the chapter he is writing, and we have our heads bent together looking over his notes. I know Cynthia is outside the room and can tell Simon does too when he looks up. We both smell the waft of petunia perfume as she glides into the room.

'Darlings! Here you are, thick as thieves and studying your notes already.'

We both stand to greet her, and she loudly makes 'mwah' sounds on either sides of our cheeks. Cynthia is wearing a bright, and I mean, bright orange kaftan with a matching turban. She busies herself making tea and we chat generally about the meeting and who will be coming.

'Well, as it's an extra meeting to discuss the author interview day, I think only the brave hearts will attend,' she says, and we both agree.

'And here is Angela coming now,' I say.

Cynthia swings around to an open doorway and raises her pencilled eyebrow.

I nod. 'I can hear the lift is in use, so she must be in her wheelchair and having a bad day.'

The lift doors open and Fen steps out pushing Angela in the wheelchair.

Fen says, 'We bumped into each other outside.'

I jump up to move the chairs aside so we can accommodate the wheelchair at the table.

Simon makes tea for the women and pours plastic cups of water from the cooler while a few other members arrive.

Darren Jenkins sits down next to me, and I give him a big smile. Darren is a young writer of non-fiction.

I figure he's mid-twenties and is a train buff. He practically lives in York Railway Museum. I've never been to the museum but after listening to Darren's accounts over the months, I feel I know the place inside and out.

Looking at Darren while he talks about his beloved trains, I see the devotion and obsession shine in his eyes. This makes me wonder if Jack, the train driver in Durham was a train spotter enthusiast and had continued his passion throughout his career? Or maybe, I muse, his passion changed from trains to women as he grew older.

Darren starts to talk about his mum who he still lives with, and I listen carefully. Darren once told Simon he'd wanted to join the fire brigade or police force but couldn't pass the medical because of his small physique. Now he works in a local supermarket stacking shelves and unloading lorries.

Cynthia says, 'Let's make a start because I'm not sure how many more are coming.'

As well as being the leader of our little group, Cynthia shows her worth in acts of kindness in organising charitable funding. She's basically a very thoughtful lady. In the past, she's sent flowers to Angela when in hospital from us all and remembers our birthdays with cards. We all receive small Christmas gifts although not expensive but welcomed all the same.

She delves into a big jazzy carpet bag and lifts out two items. I stare at the bag which reminds me of Mary Poppins and how at any minute, she'll pull out a palm plant and wall mirror.

I wipe the grin from my face and concentrate on the two items.

'As it'll be a short meeting, and before we get into our plans, I thought we could do a writing prompt for ten minutes.'

I groan. Speed writing exercises are to see what your mind can imagine by looking at an object. I'm not keen because I find it hard to write to order and quickly. Although it's popular with the others, and I know Simon is a whizz at doing this, I often struggle. I borrow some paper from Fen and bring out the pen from my shirt pocket knowing I'll have to make the best of it.

Cynthia calls out, 'Okay, everyone, ten minutes - now write!'

There's a small ship in a bottle on the table, but I chose the kaleidoscope paperweight she has brought. I look at the colours in the glass web and begin to write.

'The paperweight is so pretty, she thought looking at the blue, red, and yellow colours swirling together in the bottom of the glass. And, it had been heavy enough to do the job in hand. No, not to hold down reams of papers on her desk, but to hit him over the head with.

When he'd lunged, pinning her against the desk she had tried to shove him away, but he was a big man. With her free hand she'd grappled behind her on the desk in desperate search of something to hit him with. She had grasped the paperweight and when his face was pushed down on her chest, she had slammed it against his forehead with all her might. His weight slackened in shock but not wanting to give him a chance to recover, she smashed it again in the same place and heard him groan then slide to the floor.'

I'm amazed that I've been able to write this especially after the full-on session I spent with Michael and Sherrie this afternoon. I figure, maybe it's best to do this exercise when your mind is full of other things, and you don't have time to think about the process.

Cynthia says, 'That's it – ten minutes is up! Come on, Clive, read yours first because I know you sometimes can't get your words down quickly.'

I clear my throat and take a swig of water then read the two paragraphs aloud. My piece receives a round of applause and I can't help puffing out my chest. I'm delighted with this and appear to be the only one who chose the paperweight. Everyone else wrote a piece about the ship in a bottle. We listen to Simon's murder on the high-seas, a poem from Fen about bobbing in a boat on the blue ocean, and a brief love interlude between a captain and passenger from Angela.

I turn to Darren, but he shrugs his shoulders.

'I…I didn't manage anything today,' he says. He picks at the skin on the side of his thumb, and I can tell he's nervous. Darren often does this unless he's writing or talking about his beloved trains when he takes on a different persona altogether. As always, we reassure him that it's okay and he'll manage more next time. It's one thing I love about being part of a group. We always encourage, support and criticise in a constructive manner.

Darren wears the same mucky anorak week after week and places it precisely over the back of his chair. He peers out at everyone from thick-rimmed, round glasses. From the first week I met him, I've thought of him as a "Harry Potter" lookalike.

He scribbles continuously in a notepad and has a string bag full of train photographs. I smile knowing he'd get on well with train driver, Jack in Durham.

He looks at us and murmurs, 'Have I told you before that York is the biggest museum of its type in this country and it's only a short walk from the train station if anyone who wants to go? There's over a hundred locomotives telling the history of railways.'

We all nod good-humouredly, and Darren's slight chest swells with pride in his short-sleeved, checky shirt. His arms look like slim pencils they are so skinny, and he has the tiniest hands I've ever seen on a man. Darren's deep, brown eyes follow Simon around like a lap-dog.

He turns to Simon. 'Have I shown you my photographs of the Japanese Shrinkansen train from 2007?'

Simon raises an eyebrow at us all as Darren dips down under his chair to retrieve his string bag. The ladies and I look with pleading as if to say, please stop him getting all the photographs out yet again.

Placing a hand on Darren's shoulder, Simon says in a gentle voice, 'Oh yes, Darren, you certainly have, and it was very impressive. Why not buy an album and put all your photographs in the correct order of dates? Or the order in which you took them?'

Darren sits back up again and drops the handles of the bag. He grins. 'Hey, Si, that's a great idea – thanks.'

I see us all breathe a sigh of relief. I'm not sure what Simon will think about the abbreviation of his name, but I know he's too much of a kindly soul to object. Hmm, nicely done using great distraction techniques, I think and wink at Simon who grins.

Simon says, 'Right, thanks for that, Darren but shall we get on with the plans for our author interview day?'

Cynthia has a battered black diary on the table in front of her with what seems like hundreds of post-it notes on pages. Maybe this is her way of staying with the programme as it were.

She nods. 'Yes, so I think we all know by now there is a new author showcase happening in the library and we, the writing group have been asked to take part and help organise.'

Fen's face lights up. 'Shall we have drinks and nibbles, Cynthia?'

Cynthia claps her hands together. 'Oh, yes, Fen, what a great idea,' she says. 'Are we thinking flavoured sparkling water and cashew nuts?'

Darren quips, 'I'm not keen on cashew nuts and they're expensive. I think salted nuts will be much better because I like those.'

I see Cynthia's shoulders rise as if she's up and ready to set sail on the ship in her bottle. 'Well, Darren, I don't think decisions should be made upon personal preferences. It'll be what's best for the authors and the reputation of Harrogate library,' she says haughtily. 'And, I can assure you when it comes to high class drinks and nibbles I know best.'

Darren opens his mouth to argue but closes it smartly when Fen interrupts, 'And I can make, Spring rolls, prawn toasts, and chicken wings.'

He mutters shyly, 'Oooh, lush, Fen. Now I like all of those.'

Fen pats his hand in a motherly fashion which makes me smile. Darren obviously brings out her maternal side.

116

I know she has a big family and spends much of her days cooking for them all.

Cynthia smirks in triumph. 'So, that's decided, we'll have bottles of sparking water, cashew nuts and Fen's delicacies.'

Angela, who has been quiet throughout the session now says, 'I could get my son who works in IT to make us posters and fliers to distribute.'

I see Cynthia nod in pleasure and pat Angela's hand in thanks.

'Whoopie,' I say and grin. 'Let me know when they're ready and I'll put some out in York when I'm doing my historic tours.'

Cynthia nods. 'Right, that's great. So, we'll have two authors in the afternoon to interview and I wondered if Simon and Clive would like to do this? Maybe take an author each?'

I look at Simon and we both smile at each other. 'Yes, Cynthia, we can do this,' I say. 'And we'll organise the book signings afterwards.'

She beams at us. 'That's marvellous and perhaps we should do a short introductory speech before the two interviews?'

I sigh. Here's something else to set my pulse racing and my knees knocking. 'Well, I'll be okay asking questions and making conversation,' I say. 'But I'm not the best at speaking in front of an audience.'

Simon grins. 'Me, neither,' he says, and looks at me. 'I'll toss you for it?'

Darren produces a coin from his pocket and flips it up into the air.

I call, 'Heads, and I have to do it!'

The coin lands on its tail and I chortle while Simon groans.

Chapter Sixteen

I'm in the office eager to write up my notes from the visit to Michael and Sherrie. I begin to note down as much of Michael's account as I can remember which is easy because I've always had a good memory, unlike Barbie who struggles to recall what we did last month.

Feelings of sadness sweep through me as I type. My throat feels scratchy, and I stare down at my hands on the keyboard. When I write how Michael's Dad had stood in the garden doing nothing, I stop typing and clench my fists.

What a worthless specimen of mankind he really is, I think. I'd like to write this down, but don't because these records must be accurate, and Michael hadn't actually said this. It's only my opinion.

I finish up Michael's memories of the fire that night and further down the page, I write the questions that he has asked. Headlining a note for myself to either speak to Geoff or dig out information about life insurance and newspaper story payments.

I push my chair back and walk around the office in circles. I can't imagine the fear if I was woken up from sleep by the smell of smoke and the cracking noise of flames. I think of our house and know my first action would be to drag Barbie from our bed, get us both downstairs, and outside to safety. This also makes me wonder when the last time our fire alarms had been tested and decide to buy new ones for the whole house tomorrow.

I go through Michael's movements in my mind. I imagine him staggering from the sofa in the lounge and through to the hall where the fire was raging behind him at the front door. I can see him full of terror, coughing and spluttering, and fleeing outside from the back door into the garden. I grind my back teeth. Michael had found his dad was already out there.

This begs the question, how was Peter outside on his own? If he had woken up to the smell of smoke, as he'd originally claimed, why didn't he wake his wife, son, and daughter upstairs before running downstairs. And how could he leave Michael on the sofa knowing full well that he was there? I grimace and answer my own question because he was a coward. He'd obviously just thought of himself and ran outside without caring a jot about his family.

I sit back down at my desk and begin to copy Peter's account of the fire, his actions from the court case records, and his story from the newspaper I've put together. Typing quickly, I highlight the discrepancies in Peter's account from Michael's, marking them in red of which there are many.

I also make a list of questions I want to ask Michael when I next visit to double check Peter's inconsistencies. Some background family history would help to build up a picture. Who was his mam and what was their marriage like in the early days? I'd also like to know about Michael's siblings and his Grannie. Their standing in the neighbourhood, and information about the Indian men who'd tried to fight their way inside to rescue the rest of his family.

With the newspaper article on the screen, I stare at a photo of Peter. Michael doesn't look much like him at all. There are no photographs of his mam or siblings, and

I suppose Michael won't have any either because they would have all gone up in flames that night.

In Peter's story to the newspaper, he had said things about Michael which, even back in those politically incorrect days, were offensive. Peter had called his son a simpleton which is a dreadful word to use. Peter had said, 'His best son had died upstairs in the fire and that his daughter was his little princess.'

Which makes it obvious to me that Peter liked or loved two siblings above the other.

His next sentence reads, 'Michael will snap one day. His mam spoilt him rotten as a little boy, in fact, I wouldn't be surprised if Michael ended up a queer!'

At the end of the story, he'd tried to shift the blame onto his son by telling the reporter Michael had been obsessed with fire from being a little boy – he'd been fascinated by flames and lived for bonfire night in November.

This guy is better off dead, I reckon, because he's a monster. And if I was religious, which I'm not, I hope he burns in hell which would give him a taste of what he'd done to his family.

In an effort to rid my mind of awful thoughts, I Google the words, theft through fraud which Sherrie asked about. I learn the definition is, a person who intentionally and purposely obtains property belonging to someone else through deceptive tactics.

This makes me think about Peter's new wife. I suppose she will have entitlement to all monies he's left after his death which would include life insurance. If they hadn't married, Michael would have more chance of challenging this. However, from reading the articles about Peter, I figure he wasn't the type of man to take out insurance. The house which burned to the ground had been a council house, so they would have been re-housed after the fire.

I write this on my list of questions and discover nowadays you can get up to £10K for your story in a newspaper. How much they paid in the 1990s is a question which Geoff may be able to answer. Speak of the devil, I think as Geoff wanders into the office, and I realise it's lunch time.

'Hey, Clive,' he says plonking himself down at his desk. Wearing jeans and a green sweatshirt, he pulls the neckline away from his collarbone. 'God, it's muggy in here.'

'Yeah, I've just finished writing up my notes from yesterday with Michael and Sherrie if you want to hear about them?'

Geoff smiles. 'Yes, of course, but let's go out and grab a pint and some lunch first.'

I nod and shuffle the papers into a pile on my desk while he walks towards the door. He turns to say, 'I'm conscious that I haven't been around much since you started and have thrown you in at the deep end, as it were.'

I get up and push my chair in towards the desk. 'Ah, that's okay, I know you're busy.'

Geoff holds open the door and gently slaps my shoulder. He laughs. 'And, a little tip, if you're going to follow someone on a Saturday morning, Clive, you need to study and know your subject well. A man like me wouldn't walk or take a bus, so you'll need a car!'

He heads off downstairs and I'm mortified that he'd seen me outside his house. My cheeks burn red. The flush spreads to the tips of my ears and sweat forms on my top lip. I follow him quickly down the stairs protesting, 'Oh, no! I'm so sorry!'

Geoff walks down the path and I hurry alongside continuing to apologise. It's only now he is striding out, that I notice Geoff has a slight limp. He stops outside The Three Tuns pub. 'Let's go in here, they do nice grub, nothing fancy but I'm starving!'

I follow him inside and stand at the bar shoving my hands inside my pockets. We choose steak pies, and while he pays and waits for drinks, I sit at a nearby table.

The pub is quiet although it is early. I feel like a nincompoop and ram my knees together under the table. This could be the end of my new career before I got started and wonder if Geoff is going to sack me? However, he doesn't seem too perturbed about my botched attempt at surveillance and has even made jokes. I fiddle with a beer mat wondering if Margaret had told him she'd been to the office and met yours truly.

Geoff returns and hands me a glass of coke which I gulp because my throat is dry. 'I feel like a prize idiot,' I say, and apologise once more.

'Hey, don't worry. I'm seeing this as a plus because you're obviously keen to absorb the business and want to improve by learning new things.'

Our food arrives and I'm not sure if I'll be able to swallow the pieces of meat, but Geoff tucks into his pie with gusto.

'And, if you'd like to learn surveillance properly, there's a training course you can go on run by The IPI

Foundation,' he says. 'It's on-line and
provides the keystone knowledge for a qualification.'

I cheer up considerably and cut a slice of pie. 'Really?'
I say, 'Well, yes, I'd love to do that.'

'Great,' Geoff says. 'You'll learn how to monitor a
subject and their activities through observation, how to
use a surveillance vehicle that blends in, pre-surveillance
scene checks, positioning, distractions, and using a
camera in an investigation, amongst other things of
course.'

He takes a long swig of his pint and I take the
opportunity to say, 'I don't know if Margaret told you,
but she came to the office and asked me to follow you,
but I refused. I'm not working for her, nor have I
accepted her money.'

Geoff smiles. 'That's good to know. My wife has never
understood anything about surveillance work, Clive or
the need for confidentiality. I've been working for
Margaret's cousin, called Jemma who lives in Glasgow.
Last month, she asked me to follow her wife, Stephanie
who she's convinced is playing around with someone
else. Jemma doesn't want anyone, not even Margaret, to
know about this failing partnership, as she sees it,' he
says, and draws his eyebrows together. 'So, part of the
assignment, along with a large amount of money, is
absolute concealment. Jemma is a property developer
and put me up in a fabulous apartment in the city while I
was trailing Stephanie. She's delighted now to have her
answers and what she does with them is up to her. I
never get involved with the result, I simply move on to
the next case.'

With this revelation, I swallow the last piece of steak pie and moan. How could I have got this impression of him so wrong? My stupid suspicious mind has added two and two together and come up with five – a huge mistake.

Geoff must think I've moaned in pleasure because he says, 'Yeah, the pies are great – aren't they?'

I smile and park up my feelings to think through later. Relaxing my knees and shoulders, I breathe a sigh of relief. 'Thanks for being so understanding about Saturday,' I say.

He nods. 'It's not a problem, Clive. It shows me you have an inquisitive mind and some of it is my fault for not being around. You were bound to be curious about what I do,' he says. 'I've got so used to behaving like a spy from MI5 that I forget about ordinary life.'

I chortle knowing he's trying to put me at ease which is working.

Devouring his pie, Geoff says, 'You know, way back from the 1930s, PI officers and investigators have had a poor reputation through doing sleazy, underhand cases, and charging large fees for small amounts of investigation. I never want my business to have this standing and am striving to make it professional, fair, and gain good recommendations.'

I can see the sincerity in his eyes and how much this business means to him. I smile. 'Well, from what I've seen in the office, so far, I think you're doing just that.'

He nods and continues, 'Most PIs reckon the government licensing course is necessary, but it doesn't automatically set you up for success in the job.

Apprenticing and practice will help more alongside an understanding of how the PI industry works.'

'It sounds exciting,' I say. 'And yes, I'd love to go forward with all of this.'

Geoff licks his lips and places his knife and fork together on the plate. 'Well, actually, you're doing some of the apprentice learnings already by meeting and talking with clients face to face who are seeking justice. Typically, we find proof of wrongdoing and try to fix the client's situation which can be done by interviewing witnesses and gathering intelligence.'

I smile and drain my coke from the glass.

Geoff pushes back his chair. 'Come on, let's head back to the office and you can tell me all about Michael and Sherrie on the way.'

***

While Barbie is washing dishes after our dinner that evening, I pull myself up onto one of the red worktops in the kitchen and tell her about Geoff. I cringe telling her about my stupid surveillance and can see she wants to laugh because the corners of her lips are twitching, but she doesn't.

'Well, it sounds like you've developed some type of working relationship with him at long last. And yes, I agree, if he'd been around more your imagination wouldn't have run riot, but it still doesn't explain Margaret's accusations about leaving the force through dodgy dealings, does it?'

My mobile rings, I jump down and head into the lounge. Grabbing it from the coffee table, I see Rodger's name on the screen and smile. Right on cue, I think and swipe the screen. 'Hey, how goes it?'

Rodger apologises for not getting back to me sooner after talking to Paul on Saturday. We chat about his new exhibition and the neighbourhood watch meetings. I mention the fire alarms in our houses, and he agrees to add the subject to the next agenda.

'So,' he says. 'You want to know about Margaret Smithson our neighbour?'

I smile knowing he'll give me a full description and account of his knowledge. 'Yes please, Rodger.'

'Well, Margaret was a little strange growing up and her father had been worried. She was often in trouble at school for making up fanciful notions and telling lies about friends.'

'Oh, really?'

'Yes, now as far as I can remember, at university, it was something about a great looking guy and a leggy blonde. Margaret had said he'd cheated on her, but the guy categorically stated that he hadn't even gone out with her and didn't know who she was. Her father died in his early 60s and left the business and house to Margaret hoping she'd make a go of it. And from what I've seen since his death, she has excelled herself and made a great job of running the business. I believe it's gone from strength to strength.'

I smile with my mind buzzing at this information. 'Okay, Rodger, thanks for that, and what about Geoff?'

I imagine Rodger rubbing his chin with his podgy fingers. 'Well, I don't know Geoff at all, and this is only gossip mind, but I heard he'd been in the police force and had been badly beaten up. And, after months of rehab and counselling, he decided it was something he couldn't hack anymore and left to start his own PI business with easier jobs.'

I thank Rodger and we end the call. Mystery about Geoff solved, I think and nod in satisfaction. I have solid reasons now to quell my doubts.

As we head upstairs to bed, I think of Michael and double check all the plugs are pulled out of sockets and all appliances are switched off. Climbing into bed next to Barbie, I shiver and cuddle into her back. First thing tomorrow, I'm going to buy new alarms and cut that blooming grass.

Chapter Seventeen

Sitting on the train back to Harrogate, I think through what happened at lunch with Geoff. Barbie's advice had been to put it behind me and start afresh, which I intend to do. I've learned a valuable lesson and have cautioned myself against letting my imagination run riot again.

I know now that he wasn't having an affair with Jemma. He hadn't been sacked from the force but left of his own accord after a serious attack. Which is probably why he limps with a slight disability although it obviously doesn't stop him doing his job. He must have a lot of courage to come back into this line of work after being attacked while other men might have taken a safer type of role. However, I'm learning fast that being a PI certainly isn't an office-based easy ride.

Margaret could have made up stories about dodgy dealings if she has a history of fabricating the truth. Going forward I'll only deal with the facts and won't pay attention to the rantings of an aggrieved wife.

Our relationship in the office is much better than what it was, and Barbie is right, we're working together more smoothly. I've put the train fares onto an expenses form and filled in the request to do the online PI course which I'm looking forward to immensely. I've bounced ideas of Geoff and he's helped with Sherrie's questions. He agrees that Peter Davies was a monster of a guy, although his language was a lot more colourful than mine.

I'm growing to like Geoff now as a man. He is kind, and I can tell is proud of his professionalism in the field of private investigations. He wants to give value to his clients and make sure they get the best possible outcome, which in turn, makes them feel they've got some kind of justice.

I reckon, this is a great opportunity if I want to make a career of being a PI. The salary is good, and Geoff has already hinted at a raise if I continue to progress and take on more cases. I grimace, and if I don't make a fool of myself again.

Plus, if the business grows with both of us working cases, Geoff has hinted I could work full time. It's more interesting than the travel agency, which I'd always thought of as a stop gap, and stretches my mind. It makes me think and I reckon there'll be more time in between shifts to write. It's the biggest opportunity I've had since turning eighteen when I left the offenders' institution.

My mind goes back to that time and how my friend in the institution had been from York. His father was a builder and they'd lived in a five bedroomed house. He took me in and gave me work as a labourer. I'd worked twelve hours a day and studied English at night classes which is where I met my first wife, Sarah. She'd been on the same course and was a nurse, therefore had the salary to get a mortgage. We married and bought the house on Victor Street. Shortly after this, I got the job in a travel agency, but had never thought this was my life-long career.

The train pulls into Harrogate and heading through the station, I grin. Perhaps being a PI is the new career I've been looking for without realising.

I knock on Michael and Sherrie's flat door after a neighbour from upstairs has let me through the main front door.

Michael opens it wide. 'Hey, nice to see you, Clive, come in and I'll get us a drink,' he says.

I follow him into the kitchen. Michael seems like a different guy today. He's dressed in tailored trousers and a cream dress shirt which I can tell are very good quality. These wouldn't have been cheap which makes me wonder how much a porters' salary is at the hospital, and how he can afford this level of dress. Plus, rent for these flats in the centre of Harrogate will be expensive.

I accept a glass of coke and we make small talk about the warm weather and his shift patterns which make it possible for him to see me today. When we walk back into the lounge, I look around the room.

Michael says, 'Sherrie isn't here at the moment – she's gone out shopping for groceries but won't be too long.'

He settles in his chair like last time, but sits back and crosses his legs, picking a miniscule piece of fluff from the crease of his trousers. His shoulders which were rounded and slumped last week are pulled back today as though he's extraordinarily proud of himself for some reason.

I place my mobile onto the coffee table and ask, 'Is it okay for me to record the session?'

He smiles and nods. I notice however, that his smile doesn't quite reach his eyes. It doesn't look genuine and sincere, but more calculating in a strange way. I shake these thoughts aside and start talking.

'Okay, so I've been tallying up your account of the fire and your father's from the story he sold to the newspapers and there are some inconsistencies. I wonder if we could go through them?'

Michael folds his hands together calmly in his lap and nods. I remember how he'd pulled on his fingers in agitation last time. Is it because Sherrie isn't here? Did he somehow feel intimidated by her last time or perhaps it was because he'd just woken up from nightshift.

'Ask away,' Michael says, with a charming smile on his face.

'Well, in your dad's story there's no mention of you being asleep on the sofa, and if he knew you were there?'

I watch the change sweep across Michael. He unfolds his legs and begins to tap his shoes together. He avoids my eyes and looks out of the window. His lips move swiftly as if he's finding the right words to use. In a more strident voice, he says, 'Clive, I was definitely on the sofa! Dad and I watched a football game and when I woke it was dark so he must have switched out the lights before going up to bed.'

I smile hoping to get him back into his earlier relaxed manner. 'Hey, that's fine.'

He jerks forward in the chair and furrows his eyebrows. 'Do you not believe me, Clive?'

I nod. 'Of course, I do. I'm just trying to get everything straight in my mind so I can help you as much as possible.'

Michael sits back again and re-crosses his legs with a look of smugness around his lips almost as if to say, I'm in charge here, not you. I wonder if this is way of exerting his authority over the questions and hope I'm not making him feel as though he's in court under scrutiny.

I decide to change the subject. 'Well, Michael, can you tell me a little about your family background,' I say. 'What was your mam like and were they happily married?'

Michael shrugs. 'Well, they always seemed to be when I was little. Even though Dad didn't work, we always had more than other kids at school with clean clothes, and plenty of food and treats. Plus, he made sure there was always fun and laughter in the house. Back then he'd been my hero. Mam was a cleaner at the General Hospital in Newcastle,' he says. 'But just before the fire, I'd heard one of her friends say she was bright and bubbly at work until Dad picked her up every night then she was sullen and nervous.'

I want him to elaborate on this but figure it won't make much difference to the case and push on with my next question. 'And your siblings – what were they like?'

He sighs. 'My brother was younger than me and was fourteen when he died. He was into everything, football, boxing, and was great at maths and science at school. He wanted to go to college and become an engineer because he was good at putting things together. Although I was never included, him and Dad spent a lot of time together. My sister was twelve when she died. She was a proper girly, girl, played with dolls, wore pink all the time and went to dance classes on a Saturday morning.'

This corresponds with what Peter had said in his story and obviously Michael felt left out because his dad spent more time with his brother. 'I never had brothers and sisters so can't imagine what that was like.'

'Well, I haven't got any now, so we're the same, Clive, all on our own.'

I smile. 'Oh, but you have Sherrie, and I have a great fiancé, called Barbara.'

I shuffle uneasily on the leather sofa at the wily look in his eyes. It's as though he's hatching a plan in his mind. I push on with my last question. 'And what were your neighbours like? You said previously they came to help?'

He nods. 'Yeah, that's right. Dad hated Mr Singh across the street and was convinced he'd set the house on fire after an argument over noise and parking cars. Dad was racist and called the neighbours awful names, but I liked them and went to school with their kids.'

Ah, I think and feel a shiver run up my back. I hope Michael's generation will do away with the 60s racist attitudes. I can't bear to watch old sitcoms like, "Love They Neighbour" with the English mindset. In those days, it was just an accepted outlook, but now I find it repugnant.

I ask, 'Did you read the story in the newspaper from 1990?'

Michael drains the coke from his glass and frowns. 'No, I never wanted to because it would have upset me.'

I hope he never does because it'll make him hate his dad more than he does now. From what he's told me, I can't help feeling there's more built-up emotion inside this young guy. Which would be understandable after what he's been through and is still going through. However, I feel like I've got to know him better on this visit and decide to close the interview. 'Well, Michael, that's me done so have you any other questions from last week?'

He nods. 'Did your boss say I should report Dad's confession to the police,' he asks, and then answers his own question with a frown. 'I mean, what good would it do now?'

'None,' I say. 'They wouldn't do anything because all crimes die with the person who has confessed them - they'd simply record the event. My boss will certainly inform the police for you, and it'll put you in the clear and go some way to salving your conscience.'

Michael sighs. 'And did you look into how much money Dad got for his newspaper story?'

He's asked for this twice, so I figure it's important to him and reply, 'Well, it was a council house that you lived in so there wouldn't be any house insurance as such, but he might have had contents insurance and claimed on that, I suppose.'

Michael rubs his chin with his long fingers. 'And do you know how much that would have been?'

I shake my head. 'You'd need to find out the name of the insurance company and ask them to delve back in their records. I doubt they'd tell me because I'm not family.'

He nods. 'And the newspaper amount?'

'Well, I can't tell you that exactly how much they paid back then, but nowadays if you were to sell your story to the newspapers it would be approx. £10K.'

Michael whistles between teeth and I almost see pound signs spin in his eyes. He seems obsessed with the amount of money his dad got.

However, that's his business, and it's up to him what he does about his stepmother's inheritance.

My job is to piece all of the bits of information together for him which he couldn't do when he was fifteen, and according to Sherrie he can't do now for himself, and I've done just that.

I get up to leave and smile wanting to end the session on a good note. 'Mind, I must say, Michael this is a lovely flat you've got here.'

Michael huffs his shoulders and almost pouts, 'Actually, it's an apartment not a flat!'

I mumble an apology and he insists upon showing me around. I follow him out into the hallway.

His eyes gleam. 'Yeah, Sherrie keeps the place spotlessly clean.'

Michael shows me their bedroom and throws his arm wide in a sweeping gesture, talking as though he's an estate agent giving a running commentary about their grey high-gloss furniture and the light from the huge windows.

His stride is almost cocky as I follow him into the second bedroom. This room is adjoined, and I can't think it would be a good selling point to have one bedroom lead into another. Of course, some couples may use it as office space. The room is empty apart from a big bookcase which occupies the length of the wall. Michael stands in front of it now and calls out, 'Ta-da!'

I walk up to the bookcase which appears to be full of crime, horror, and police procedure novels. 'Ahh, so you're an avid crime reader?'

'Yeah, these are my favourite authors.'

Hoping to find a common ground between us I tell him about my two books on Amazon and the entire atmosphere changes.

'OMG!' He cries. 'You're an author!'

I nod and lift out a book of a writer unknown to me and then turn it around to read the back cover. Michael is practically breathing down my neck. 'I don't know this author,' I say. 'Is it a good read?'

He goes into a dramatic explanation of the book, and I smile. 'Ah, the writer has obviously got you hooked which is what I hope to do with my readers.'

I see him swallow hard and lick his lips in front of my face now. 'I'm going to find your books on Amazon right now and order them,' he says. 'A...and would you come back and sign them for me, pleaseee?'

At the childish exaggeration of the word, please, I take a step back finding the closeness and his warm breath on my face unpleasant. Geoff's words come back to me about not getting emotionally involved and moving on to the next case.

I don't want to give him my mobile number and say, 'Just ring the office and leave a message. And if you like whodunnit mysteries, try my friend's book, he's called Simon Travis and it's a great story.'

Michael looks smitten with me. It's the only word I can find to describe the look on his face as he practically dances around in a weird besotted manner.

His voice oozes. 'So now I'll be able to say, I know Clive Thompson and he's a friend of mine!'

I head to the door and chortle. Aww, I think, fame at last.

When I turn the corner of Raglan Street, I see Sherrie walking towards me carrying three heavy bags of shopping. Instantly, I hurry to her and take two of the bags.

As we walk, she tells me, 'Thanks for coming back, Clive. Michael would be lost trying to gather the information for himself with his condition. That's why I offered to pay for your services just to put his mind at rest. And now he'll know we've done everything we can to sort this matter out. You see, he's not easy with people mainly because of what happened in his childhood. But I love Michael for what he is.'

I want to say Michael is a lucky guy to have her fighting his corner but figure it might sound inappropriate. I look at her stick-thin legs in tight denim jeans and tell her briefly what's happened today. 'I figure we've done our bit now and my boss will report it to the police.'

She looks up at me with tearful blue eyes and nods. 'Now that he knows the truth, he hates his dad. And the realisation that Peter had destroyed his whole family in an act of arson for insurance money tortures him.'

'It can't be easy,' I say. 'Learning something like that must surely mess with your mind.'

We reach the bottom of the steps up to their flat and I put the two bags of shopping down for her.

'I think it has, and during the lock-downs he became a little off-kilter. But there again so did a lot of people. We kept repeating the phrase everyone was saying throughout the pandemic, "It's okay not to be okay." And at work in the hospital, we both felt a bit broken with the chaos and shocking number of deaths occurring.

I had a scream cupboard at home in our bedroom where I'd let off steam if Michael was driving me nuts.'

I remember my time during lock-down and nod. 'Yeah, me too, I used the garden shed to scream and shout, and yes, it was a very strange time for us all.'

'Well, it was the worst time for me at work, but Michael filled us both with hope that we'd get through it together - which we did.'

'And now?' I ask.

She nods. 'Well, I feel I'm back on an even keel again whereas, he's had this awful confession heaped on top of him, so I'm not sure if he's fully recovered. He's improved but he's not quite there yet,' she says, shaking her long hair. 'But I'm not giving up on him. I know he'll be able to find himself again – I just know it!'

***

Heading up to the train station I remember the horrific reports on the news of staff and patients suffering in ITU. Doctors and nurses worked blind because they knew very little about the virus and tried to save people from dying of Covid. Now, I can see first-hand how this horrible virus affected all of the ancillary staff at the hospitals too. Not only had Sherrie felt broken at work but she'd had Michael driving her crazy at home. I remember clapping outside in the garden every Thursday night for the NHS staff and know they deserve more than a round of applause.

Living through the pandemic had been a time for all communities in the UK to pull together where people cared for elderly neighbours. And where some services were closing like libraries and swimming pools, communities strived to keep them open. I'd read a government survey which showed how difficult times had truly brought out the best of us as a nation and helped to pull us through. The fact that ninety percent of elderly adults agreed they had people who were there for them if needed, spoke volumes for the strength of our communities.

Mrs Webster often says, 'We have to believe there's enough good in people to trust them to do the right thing.'

Heading into the train station, I know this is true and run along the platform to catch the train back to York. Settled in the seat, I gaze out of the window and think about the change in Michael's persona from my first visit. His expressions can change rapidly in the blink of an eye, from being happy friendly and in control, to huffy and tetchy. And as soon as I'd mentioned I'm an author, he changed to showering me with compliments.

It had been like hero worship, and I smile knowing I don't deserve such adulation. I chortle, I'm certainly not James Paterson or Peter James, well not yet anyway.

Chapter Eighteen

Michael sat cross legged on the floor in front of his beloved bookcase. He smiled knowing today had gone so much better because he'd sent Sherrie to the shops and had been alone with Clive. Which, in turn, meant he'd been in control of the session and had his boundaries in place – not Sherrie's. He'd had space and time to think through his plan.

He glanced and then tutted at the second shelf of the bookcase where Clive hadn't put the book back into its correct place. They were all in the order of when he'd read them. Not in alphabetical order like many other people would do, but there again, Michael grinned, he wasn't like other men. He was just that little bit different which is what his mam used to say.

Wistfully, he thought about Clive being an author and how he was able to write a whole book. Michael could barely write a few sentences on a bad day, but on a good day, he could manage a little more. Any type of forms, documents, or records filled Michael with dread. He hated the log sheets at work and often got someone else to fill them in for him.

Pulling his mobile from the pocket of his trousers he ordered both of Clive's novels. He stared at Clive's photograph on Amazon and felt a shiver run along his shoulders. This was his friend, Clive Thompson, the author. Michael frowned at the delivery date wishing they would arrive sooner but knew he would read them as soon as they plopped through the letterbox.

How did Clive think of these stories and all the great characters, he wondered? He loved the sound of the book set in Whitley Bay with a suspicious death on the causeway – what an imagination he must have. Michael practically drooled at the thought of opening the first page of the book.

He ran his fingers lovingly along the wood on the top of the bookcase. It was smooth, comforting and he smiled. Not a pick of dust on here because Sherrie was fanatical with cleaning the apartment. Michael reckoned she had a cleaning obsession, which perhaps came from working in the pharmacy where everything was sparkling clean. She'd often told him cleanliness reduced the risk of infections in every area of the hospital and not just the wards where the patients were. This infatuation was handy when he wanted to upset her - all he had to do was make a mess in the apartment and she couldn't bear it.

Michael knew he was a bit off kilter at the moment and was obsessing over tiny things. Although Sherrie had reassured him that he would soon be feeling better when the medication kicked-in and helped his low mood. He smiled. She was so gullible which made it very easy to hide things from her because she thought he was taking the tablets – but he wasn't.

Her parents were loaded, and they paid their rent for the apartment although Michael knew they didn't like him. One night in the kitchen, he'd heard them say, 'Sherrie, you could do so much better for yourself than Michael.' Which he hadn't like at all.

His mind wandered back to Clive's questions. Michael felt proud that he'd lead their discussion by feeding him snippets of family life before the fire. By telling Clive his mam had turned into a nervous, subdued woman, he'd hoped to push the blame of their unhappy marriage back onto his dad.

Whereas, Michael knew his mam hadn't been blameless either with her affairs. He had seen her one night standing with Mr Singh on the street corner with her arms around his neck and his hands on her backside. He'd wondered since the fire if Dad had also seen them together and that was why he hated Mr Singh. Michael didn't want Clive to know this.

His sister, the little princess had whined all of the time and caused untold trouble in the house. She'd sneak their antics to Dad who automatically blamed him and his brother. Michael had taken the brunt of the punishment because Dad had been a little scared of his brother who'd learned how to fight back. He'd seen the fear in his dad's eyes when his brother squared up to him.

Michael had also been scared of his brother although he never hurt him. If anything, he protected him both at school and at home. He remembered seeing a children's doctor with his mam when he was about twelve. Now, he knew the correct name for this doctor – he'd been a child psychologist. Michael had an excellent memory for some things especially events when he'd been with his mam. He could repeat the doctors sentences exactly because they weren't the words that anyone would ever forget.

'Michael thinks he knows everything and has a definite personality disorder. He has a low emotional status. No empathy but has bags of charm and can seduce people very easily. He even tried to manipulate me in our meeting. He's not interested in anyone else's problems but his own.'

The words, learning difficulties, had been bandied about at school, but Michael knew he didn't have this. He wasn't a slow student if it was something he loved to read like crime novels. When it came to maths and science subjects, he used the learning difficulty label to avoid homework which he thought was pointless. Michael never contradicted anyone and allowed the teachers to believe he simply couldn't complete the work. It had been a great excuse to get out of doing stuff he didn't want to do like algebra and PE.

His legs were cramping now, and he stretched them out with his back up against the bookcase. He began to tap his shoes together in a rhythm and rubbed the back of his neck at the thought of his meeting with a new line manager the next day. Another porter had put a complaint in against him claiming that Michael had bullied him into swapping his shifts on two occasions. Which he had.

Michael hated night shift and did everything possible to get out of working in the hospital at night. He hated the solitude, the dark endless corridors, the never-ending silence, the absence of staff to talk with, and above all, the eerie atmosphere if he had to take a cadaver to the mortuary.

Unbuttoning his top shirt button, Michael jumped up and began to pace around the bedroom. The thought of losing his job spooked him because he liked being a porter. He had a uniform to wear, and it was an easy job. Patients and other staff looked up to him and he was amongst people all day. He enjoyed talking to the elderly who reminded him of his grannie.

Michael had never, and still didn't enjoy solitude and his own company. He walked for miles along corridors transporting people to and from wards and departments which wasn't a problem because he was fit. Gyms and jogging or any other type of disciplined exercise wasn't for him because he hated authority and being told what to do. However, he had always been a good walker mainly because he hadn't learnt to drive. And now, there was no need for driving lessons because Sherrie took him everywhere in her car.

Michael smirked knowing he would think of a way out of the complaint at work. Maybe he would play on his imaginary learning difficulties and then back this up with a few nervy twitches and cracking of his knuckles – this often worked rather well. Managers' in the past had been cagey about tackling him further and worried they'd be criticised for ignoring his disability and poor mental health condition.

Unkind people had accused Michael of being shifty and underhand when looking for ways to get off with his misdemeanours. He'd been blamed for seeking out the vulnerability in others to take advantage for his own benefit. But Michael saw this in a different way. He knew he was clever and shrewd, not conniving – he didn't like that word – it didn't suit him.

Michael heard Sherrie coming through the main door and stopped pacing. Should he go and help with the groceries? He shook his head knowing she would manage better without him. In a way, he thought of this as another cunning decoy.

If he offered to help and made a mess, she was usually glad he hadn't, so it was a win- win situation. And she couldn't complain because it had been her choice. This confused Sherrie, bless her, but all he had to do to make amends was get her into their bed. She loved being with him. He made her squeal in pleasure, and she was like putty in his hands.

Chapter Nineteen

'Where exactly does this guy live?' I ask Geoff.

We're in his car and I'm buzzing with excitement because he's taking me on surveillance with him tonight. We leave York and head out through the borough of Harrogate. I'm learning the ropes of my new job and take a sideways glance at Geoff.

'He lives in Ripon which isn't far,' Geoff answers. 'Have you been there before?'

I shake my head watching Geoff smoothly manoeuvre his silver BMW across a roundabout. I've got butterflies in my stomach and have had since lunch time. Barbie has tried her best to calm me down, but I can't help feeling hyped-up. It's as though I'm going on a whole new adventure, which of course, I am.

'I think I've been to the cathedral many years ago but can't remember much about the town centre really.'

Geoff smiles. 'Aww, well, it's a quirky but charming little place. In fact, it's known as the smallest city in the UK.'

'Oh right, and apart from the cathedral what else is there?'

He pulls up at a junction and taps his fingers impatiently on the steering wheel. 'Not much, the cathedral is the centre really,' he says. 'But the market place has cobbled streets with small cottages and quaint shops surrounding it, and I think there's a Victorian workshop museum if you like that type of thing.'

I smile. 'Well, I'm not particularly interested but Barbie might like a run out here one day. Probably the only thing I do remember from the previous visit was the amazing stained glass windows in the cathedral with the stunning bright colours.'

He nods and concentrates upon the sat nav which is directing us out to Kangel Close where the property is we're going to stake out. I can't help smiling to myself at the words, stake-out, as if I am in the programme, "Strike" sitting next to Cormoran on a dangerous mission.

Initially, when he'd asked if I wanted to join him and learn some of the basics, I'd had to think twice. I still think following someone is an invasion of their privacy and have shied away from doing this. Other than the disastrous Saturday morning debacle at Geoff's house.

However, if I do want to be a PI and make it my new chosen career it'll be a necessity and a regular part of the job. I reckon if I learn the ropes professionally from Geoff, it will help to make my mind up one way or another if this is for me or not.

I've heard that PIs sometimes break into properties to get the information they want which often antagonises the police, but Geoff has a strict protocol not to do this. Although, he's always determined to find out the truth even if he puts his life at risk. Which, I gulp, sounds a little scary to me now. However, most of the time, family or friends give him permission to do these things, and I know Geoff is never under a legal obligation to finish the case – he can always drop it anytime he sees fit.

Geoff had given me the brief when he'd asked me to come, and I re-read the details while he is looking for a parking space. We've been approached by a forty year old teacher called Paul Dobson living in Ripon who thinks his wife is having an affair with another teacher at a primary school where they both work.

Paul had told Geoff that he's suffered humiliating remarks in the staff room from other colleagues who obviously know about the clandestine affair. He'd seen first-hand what he described as furtive looks between his wife and the head of science called Tom Clarke. Therefore, Paul has asked Geoff to follow her and get concrete proof that she's seeing Tom so he can apply for a divorce.

I figure, if I put myself in Paul's shoes and successfully gain proof his wife is cheating on him then doing this surveillance will be vindicated. Of course, as Barbie had said, 'You don't know what their marriage is like and, you don't know anything about him. For all you know he could beat her every night of the week or be having affairs himself.'

And I know she's right.

Geoff smiles. 'I class these divorce surveillances as my bread and butter cases because they keep the business ticking over and I can do them quickly without spending a lot of time,' he says. 'Which means I can concentrate on more complex cases like suspicious deaths, relatives challenging inheritance, missing criminals and cold cases.'

I nod and ask, 'Cold cases?'

'Yeah, the public know from watching TV about the advances in DNA and cold cases the police have re-examined. So, relatives have contacted me to look into them,' he says, pulling his shoulders back. 'As opposed to what people see in the programmes, I don't want to be scoffed at by the police but want to work alongside them by helping bring criminals to justice.'

My interest is even more piqued and look forward to investigating these cases with Geoff. There's so much to learn going forwards that it makes my mind whirl. He parks a few doors up from the stone-faced detached house which is on a corner plot. I look around at other properties on the close and figure these must sell for around £500K at least. It's an affluent area and within walking distance of the town centre and cathedral.

'So, here we are then,' Geoff says.

I reckon he must have read my mind when he says, 'Well things must have changed since my school days. I wouldn't have thought head of science teachers were making enough money to buy properties around here?'

I nod. 'Yeah, but there again, there's lots of other reasons or ways that people have money nowadays,' I say. 'Life insurance, lottery wins, inheritance etc.'

Geoff smiles in agreement. He leans over to the back seat and grabs a small leather bag. Opening the zip, he pulls out his camera. It's a black Nikon with what Geoff has already told me has a super-zoom lens. I'm impressed as he removes the cap, fiddles with the lens, and aims it at the side window proposing the shot and image he'll hope to achieve.

'So,' he says. 'Apparently, Mrs Dobson drives a cream coloured mini and she's told Paul that she's out with friends at eight tonight for dinner.'

I glance down at the clock on the dashboard which reads just after nine. Dusk is falling and there's very little light left now. I look up at the house and notice it is in darkness. 'There's no lights on at all and no sign of a mini?'

Geoff shakes his head. 'You're right and this could all be a waste of time if they are simply out for dinner with friends,' he says. 'Do you want to get out and have a look at the back of the house in case she's parked up there?'

I nod and undo my seat belt.

'By the way, I'm loving the old brown tracksuit bottoms and scruffy trainers,' he says, and laughs.

I look at his neat black sweater and black trousers. Even though he'd said to wear old dark coloured clothes, I still feel under-dressed. 'But you said old clothes?'

Geoff squeezes my arm. 'I'm only joking – you look the part and will blend in with ordinary passers-by.'

I climb out of the car and know this isn't true. First, if I did live around here, I'd be wearing more expensive casual clothes like Geoff's, and second, if any of the neighbours do see me, they'll be suspicious because I look scruffy like a thug from a rundown estate and will probably call the police.

Note to oneself, invest in better quality designer clothes from a charity shop. I push my hands into the side pockets of my brown hoodie jacket and saunter casually around to the back of the house. At the back of the property, there's a tall fence around the garden but it has a narrow opening to a driveway where I can see two cars parked. One just happens to be a cream coloured mini. Bingo, I think and grin, she's here.

I continue to walk on past the house and back up to the corner to Geoff's car. Opening the passenger door, I slide back inside and give him two thumbs up.

'Yep, she's there with her mini, and there's a light on in what looks to be like a dining room with bifold doors leading outside although these are closed.'

Geoff grins. 'Brilliant deductions, Sherlock.'

I chortle. 'Well, Dr Watson, how are we going to get inside?'

Geoff looks up and under the top of the windscreen. 'I'm figuring we get up onto the roof because there's one of those trendy new skylights above which must be the kitchen,' he says. 'We'll try and find a drainpipe or a ladder. It's amazing what people leave lying around!'

I gulp and can almost feel my knees knock at the very thought of the roof. But, I'm here now and I am not going to back out. If Geoff, who I figure is older than me with a limp can climb up there, then so can I.

He turns and hands me what looks like a black balaclava. 'Really?' I say, raising my eyebrow.

He grins. 'Oh, yeah.'

We get out of the car. There's no one at all on the street and we hurry around to the back of the house. Amazingly, there's what looks like an old fashioned metal fire escape on the side of the house. I can see a couple of rungs which are rusted and broken, but Geoff goes up gingerly testing his feet on it first. He whispers, 'It's okay – just tread carefully.'

With shaking legs and sweaty palms on the handrail I follow him slowly. He misses out the two rusty rungs and lifts his leg up higher testing out the next one. It's strong enough to hold him and I take a big sigh of relief. I know I weigh less than him so follow his lead with my thoughts in a whirl.

I figure it's best not to think too much about what I'm doing but decide to be careful and stay safe.

Geoff scrambles up onto the roof now and creeps along the edge to the skylight where he leans up against the height of it and stands still waiting for me. I've caught up with him now and chant to myself, don't look down, don't look down.

We stay still and quiet then Geoff squeezes my arm. He whispers, 'Try and get your legs into a relaxed and comfortable position because we might be here a while.'

I do as he bids. It's eerily quiet and I look up to the stars in the dark sky. I spit out a bit of fluff from inside the balaclava and shrug my shoulders. Well, I think, sitting on a roof top is certainly different to channel hopping on the TV of an evening. I know already I'm learning loads from Geoff and things like this won't be on the course.

The skylight is aluminium, and the colour seems to glisten in the dark. I look down into the kitchen at the sparkling new oak cupboards, matching table and high-back chairs with shiny black worktops. The lights are off, but there's neon strip lights along the counters which give enough light to see into the room.

Barbie would love a kitchen like this, I reckon. And although I've got my qualms about what I'm doing, if I do decide to be a PI, I could afford to buy her one of these beauties, which makes me smile.

Now we are in a settled position, and even though I'm sitting on a roof top, I give myself a moment to think about this. It felt a bit sordid at first but exhilarating at the same time, and I'm loving the escapade. What we're doing to get a result overrides the privacy issue, and I try to think of it as just another case like Geoff does. Mrs Dobson is obviously guilty of being here without her husband, but it could just be a drink and meal out although there's no sign of other friends with cars.

I watch him lift up the camera and get into a position where he aims it downwards through the glass. He fiddles about with the strap while I shiver feeling cold and wishing I'd worn a thicker jumper. Just as I wonder how long we'll have to wait, I know the Gods are with us when suddenly, I hear Geoff whistle gently through his teeth.

And here she comes, I think watching Mrs Dobson sashay into the kitchen wearing a short black negligee. Did women still wear these nowadays? Now I can see quite clearly Mrs Dobson is cheating on Paul, and I have no prick of conscience.

I watch her open the large American fridge door and lift out a bottle of champagne. In a second, Tom is behind her wrapping his arms around her waist. He's a big guy in shorts and a white vest and nuzzles into the back of her neck. I hear Geoff click his camera.

'Got you,' he whispers. 'I'll take another just in case.'

And then I feel rather than see his foot slip a little. Geoff grabs onto the side of the skylight to stop himself from falling. We can both tell the noise was enough to be heard inside when Tom and Mrs Dobson look up startled.

'Run!' he shouts.

As if the devil is behind me, I hurry back along to the top of the fire escape. My heart is thumping against my ribcage. Rather than take the rungs carefully, I put my hands on both of the rails and slide down quickly landing on the ground with a thud. Geoff is a second behind me copying my actions and we flee around the corner back to the car.

I'm gasping for breath, and by the time we reach the car, Tom is flying out through the front door yelling at us. Pulling open the passenger side door, I glance over my shoulder - he looks scary and is built like a body-builder.

Geoff is now inside the car and turns on the ignition before I've actually shut the door. He rams his foot down and we race off down the road. I look out of the back window. Tom is still chasing after us waving his fist, but I can see there's no way he'll catch up with the car. I whip off the balaclava, wipe the sweat from my forehead with the sleeve of my hoodie, take a huge breath in and let it out slowly.

I look at Geoff and mutter, 'Jeez, that was a close call.'

Geoff bellows in laughter. 'Paul didn't tell me that Tom is built like a bloody bull-dozer!'

Chapter Twenty

At work, I look at the spreadsheets and record my expenses. I'm gobsmacked at how much Geoff got paid for our stint on the roof from Paul. I notice there's also £250 extra in my wages for the week which Geoff has laughingly called danger money. Whoopie, I think knowing it would take me weeks to make this money in the travel agency or doing historical tours.

On the front of my desk is a small name-plate Geoff had made. It's black with the words, Clive Thompson, PI Assistant, written in gold lettering. I pick it up and run my fingers over the front. It makes me feel as though I belong somewhere. It says, yes, this is my place in the office and where I work now.

I sit back in the chair and remember being on the roof, the excitement of the escapade, and Geoff's approval of the way I'd handled myself.

'I think you've got a natural flair for this work, Clive,' he'd said driving back to York. 'And you're nifty on your feet which always helps. I'd never have thought of sliding down that rickety fire escape the way you did. You think on your feet, as the saying goes, which is great!'

I'd been delighted with his praise but when I reached home, I chose to tell Barbie a version of the truth because I don't want her to worry whilst I'm on surveillance. Not that I think it's going to be particularly dangerous because Geoff has already said the night in Ripon was a one-off. Often, he can use an open window, or wait for hours in his car, or trail people walking around through the day. It just happened that Mrs Dobson had the dinner excuse planned with friends to meet her lover and had been too good of an opportunity to miss. Therefore, I very much doubt I'll be scaling roofs again and being chased by a huge body-building man down the road. The other surveillance Geoff has mentioned sounds much less hazardous and more practical.

I think of science teacher, Tom and am shocked that he was such a big strapping young guy. My impression of teachers was small weedy men with glasses, dressed in checked trousers and knitted cardigans. I smile at the image but know the evening could have ended very differently if he'd caught up with us. Also, I'm glad I was wearing the balaclava, therefore Tom will never be able to trace me, that's if I'm ever in Ripon again.

Going forward, I've learnt it's best to look at the area where surveillance is to take place on street maps and Google. You can tell what the area is like by property prices. If it's an upmarket place, then yes, I'll need dark but decent clothes not the scruffy trainers and old hoodie I'd worn. This attire would fit better up near York station where it's not as salubrious.

Success in surveillance, is all in the groundwork, Geoff keeps telling me and he's right. Note to oneself, Geoff knows what he's doing and I'm learning from the best. I write up notes about our surveillance knowing Geoff will drop off the photographs to Paul of Mrs Dobson in Tom's kitchen wearing her negligee. I reckon, Paul is in for a shock when he sees them, but I suppose his wife could wear the negligee at home and he won't be at all surprised.

Barbie howled in laughter when I told her about the black lace attire. She's often said I'm very naïve when it comes to women and their wily ways, and I figure she's got me in one. I can't understand why women or men for that matter, would want to dress up in costumes. There's nothing wrong with our bodies in the natural naked state. It's a beautiful thing to see, well, Barbie's is anyway.

Knowing I'll not get much work done if I go down the route of thinking about her body, I push the delicious thoughts aside and pick up a message from Geoff.

He'd been into the office before I arrived and left me two things. First, a mobile work phone with a tracking device and his number on speed dial one if I ever need him quickly.

And second, a handwritten note, 'Michael has rang the office to ask if you'll drop by and sign your books for him. Apparently, he loved them, as did I, Clive, and they're taking pride of place on his bookshelf.'

Who could refuse this request with such admiration, and I grin. I love recommendations about my work. It's a tremendous feeling to know someone has read and enjoyed my thoughts, words, and characters woven into the story. Although in the past, tributes have been from reviews on Amazon, which are great to read, but to have personal acclaim is so much better. Knowing I'm going to meet Angela in the library to collect the posters and leaflets this afternoon I decide to call in to see Michael on the way back.

***

Barbie has just dropped me off in the library car park and I swing around at the call of my name. I see Angela is in a car with her husband who I've met before.

I hurry over to them. 'Hey, how it going?' I say but can tell by Angela's face she is in pain. Her usual smiling blue eyes aren't as smiley today and I sigh.

'I'm not having a good day,' she says. 'So, forgive me if I don't come inside.'

'Angela, you shouldn't have come out!' I stress. 'We could have made it another day or Simon would have called to your house to pick them up.'

I look to her husband who shrugs his shoulders as if to say she won't listen. He reaches across Angela and hands me the posters which are rolled up with an elastic band to secure them in place. I tuck these under my arm and take the brown A4 folder which are the leaflets.

Angela says, 'I've done you ten of the posters and fifty leaflets for York. Simon and Cynthia have the same to distribute here in Harrogate.'

It looks like saying this sentence has worn her out. I frown. This horrible MS disease is so incapacitating especially for a young person and don't know how she copes. I can see the same sadness in her husband's kind face I'm feeling.

'Okay, thanks so much for these, but please go home to bed and rest up,' I say. 'We need you better for the event because it won't be the same without you.'

She nods and smiles while her husband turns on the ignition and slowly pulls out of the car park. I follow them out onto the footpath kicking at a pebble as I go. Why her, I fume, in fact, why does anyone have to suffer like this? I can only hope she is better for the author interviews which she's done so much to help plan and organise.

Walking along to Raglan Street, I pull back my shoulders and stand outside Michael and Sherrie's flat. No, I correct myself, their apartment. I must remember this because Michael seemed vexed when I didn't get it right before. I press the intercom and can't help wondering which Michael I will see today. Nervy, tetchy Michael or cocky, composed Michael.

He calls hello through the intercom, and I push open the door. He's waiting for me with their door ajar and ushers me inside. There's a strange odour coming from him as he holds open the door in a tatty green track suit. I can tell the smell is from his armpits and wonder when he showered last? I follow him along the hall into the lounge deciding it is the former Michael I'm presented with today. He looks pale and unwell. His eyes are dull and gone is the self-assured manner as he slumps down into his chair.

There's clutter around the chair. Used tissues, an empty cup and glass, magazines, a newspaper, and a half-eaten sandwich on a plate. It looks to me as though he hasn't been out of the chair for a while.

I sit opposite him and smile. Paperback copies of my two books are on the coffee table opened at the forward page. There's a silver parker pen next to them. 'Hey, this looks great,' I say. 'And you've got them both ready for me?'

He nods. 'Yeah, I've been off sick from work for a couple of days.'

I can tell the way he wriggles his toes in bobbly grey socks that he is hesitant to say why, or indeed anything more. I sigh knowing I'm not here on a professional basis today and don't have any questions to ask.

I look around for Sherrie but decide not to mention her absence. 'Aww, I'm sorry to hear that - hopefully you'll feel better soon.'

I sit nearer to the table and pick up the pen. Choosing my oldest book out of the two which is set in London, I say, 'Now, shall I make it out to Michael, or do you want your full name?'

A light comes on behind his eyes and he leans forward. 'Just Michael, thanks.'

I smile and write, 'Thanks for visiting my world, Michael. I'm thrilled that you've enjoyed the novel. Best wishes, Clive Thompson.'

I hand it over to him and watch him read. His cheeks flush red and for the first time since I arrived, he smiles. 'Hey, that's great, Clive,' he says. 'I do feel like I'm a friend in your world now - could ring you for a chat sometime?'

Trying to veer him away from asking for my mobile number, I say, 'Have you been to London before?'

He shakes his head abruptly and gabbles, 'Oooh, no, but I loved the setting – is it really like that down there?'

I'm signing my next novel, Death at the Caravan Park, with the same message and shrug. 'I've no idea about London because I've never been before. I got a lot of descriptions from Google.'

'Really,' he asks. 'I thought you'd have to know the place to write about it?'

I nod. 'Most authors do, so that's why I set the second one in Whitley Bay because I know local places very well and it was much easier to write.'

I look at him with his head bent reading my second message even though it's the same as the first.

My heart goes out to this mixed up young guy. He's certainly been through the mill, both in his past and again last month after his dad's confession. Life can be hard for some people, in fact many people, I think and remember Angela in the car park. Michael is suffering as much although it's not a physical illness but a psychological one which can be just as debilitating in its own way.

Carrying my books, he scuttles through to the spare bedroom asking me to join him which I do. It's only when I enter the room that I see the big sabre sword on the wall above the bookcase. I must have missed seeing this last time I was here. It's a beautiful object creating an amazing scene on the plain wall.

There's a space at the front of the bookcase and Michael proudly stands my books there with the covers facing us. They're taking centre stage and I grin.

'And look,' he says, puffing out his slim chest. 'I've installed a little light behind here.'

He bends down and clicks on the light. It's startling because it shows up my covers beautifully especially the dark picture of a street in London.

'Wow, Michael, that's terrific, thank you so much.'

His face brightens even more, and he looks much better. 'And these are Simon's books,' he murmurs.

The books are on the top of the bookcase in a cardboard delivery sheaf, and I smile.

Michael continues, 'They've just arrived from Amazon this morning and I'm going to start reading them today.'

I nod. 'Simon will be so pleased. I'll tell him when I see him at the writing group.'

Michael smiles. 'Ah, so you're in a writing group?'

'Yes, we meet just across the road in the library.'

Cynthia has given us all a guest ticket to the event and originally, I'd figured on bringing Barbie but it's not quite her thing. I know she'll probably be bored listening to even more authors banging on for a couple of hours. Laughingly, she often tells me that listening to me is quite enough.

Barbie has already invited some of her food-tech friends to visit the newly opened Crimple Garden Centre on the outskirts of Harrogate. She's shown me the website and it looks huge with an amazing restaurant and gift shop. I know she'll be there most of the day looking at produce and tasting.

Michael looks like he's never been invited to anything before. Apart from Sherrie, I get the impression he's not had much attention in his sorry little life. Especially, from his grotesque father.

Making a quick decision, I pull out the ticket for the event from the back pocket of my jeans. 'Actually, we're having an author interview event soon - would you like to come along?'

I hand him the ticket and hear him gasp. He looks down at the ticket and I notice the slight tremble in his long fingers. Michael is holding the ticket as though it's an invitation to Buckingham Palace.

'Well, that's if you're not at work?'

The smile on his face reaches from one ear to another. He looks back up at me. 'I'll make sure I'm not,' he says, and raises an eyebrow. 'And you want me to come along with you both?'

I nod. 'I think you'll enjoy the event. Simon and I will be asking another two authors questions about their books – their names are on there.' I say and point to the ticket.

He smooths a finger over the edge which Angela's son has cleverly embossed with gold – they look very professional. Note to oneself, make sure your thank Angela properly in the group and ask Cynthia to buy her son a gift of thanks.

Michael looks so pleased it brings a lump to my throat.

'Oh, wow,' he says. 'I'll tell Sherrie all about it when she comes back from work.'

I expand with more details about the event. He's full of questions and longing to meet Simon. I unroll the posters and we look at them together. They're cleverly printed in bright eye-catching colours with a great photo of the Royal Pump Room Museum in the centre. It's not where the event is to be held, but represents Harrogate, therefore people will know where to travel for the day. I tell Michael how I'm going to put them in York on the tour route and Simon will put the posters up in strategic places here in Harrogate.

Michael nods. 'Would you like me to put one up on the notice board in the hospital?'

I'm bowled over by his generosity in the midst of him not feeling well and hope he'll go back to work before the event occurs. I thank him profusely and pull out a poster from the scroll. Giving it to him, I head towards the front door and call goodbye.

Chapter Twenty One

On my way home, I read a message from Tommy Sanderson who is the tour company manager I often work for in York centre. Since I started working with Geoff, the tours have taken a back seat, but my old adage of how to survive financially kicks-in, and know I always need a plan B in life.

He says, 'Apologies for the short notice, Clive, but we wondered if you could step in and do the ghost trail this evening?'

My shoulders slump. I'd hoped to have the evening free to write the plot for my next novel which I'm going to show to the publishers at the festival. However, I think of the tips I could make and how it would add to our wedding fund. I reply, 'Yes, that's no problem at all.'

Hurrying through the lounge, I check the weather forecast on my iPad. Dry but warm, it tells me, and I work out the trail accordingly. If it rains, I organise places under cover and shop doorways to talk to the customers and tell them my stories. This won't be a problem tonight, I think and smile. I have a light-bulb moment knowing I'll be able to put up posters and do leaflet drops for our event whilst I walk around York.

Barbie is upstairs packing my holdall to stay at Simon's house and her own bag to stay in Durham for the weekend. I call upstairs and let her know about the tour.

She shouts down the stairs, 'Have fun!'

I click onto the tour website to re-check the details of the trail because it's been a while since I've done this tour called "Silence in York Shambles".

With the roll of posters under my arm and a packet of blue tack, I head to the pick-up point at St. Helen's Square. The tour hasn't changed and is described as York's Mystery Trail.

The details explain that it is a walking tour which navigates past the best historical landmarks that York has to offer. It has the perfect route plotted-out to make sure customers see all the highlights inside the city walls. York Minster, The Golden Fleece Inn, The Shambles, and more hidden gems.

When I reach the square, there are around twenty people standing in front of the Mansion House which is a beautiful Georgian building in red and white stone pillars. It's the home of the Lord Mayor of York during their term of office.

I step up to the group and introduce myself. 'Okay, everyone, let's get going on this thrilling journey around the city,' I say, and sweep my arm dramatically around in a circle. 'So, here we are in the square where the lights are switched on at Christmas, and we always have our beautiful big tree. In the 1700s this square was the main departure point for two stagecoaches to London, so I guess it was their early bus station!'

There's a slight snigger from the women but I know at this stage the group are singular in their interactions and won't begin to communicate with me, and each other, until later when we head through the city.

I usher everyone forward along Stonegate to walk up to the minster. I chat easily with two middle-aged women who are closest to me while keeping my eye on an older couple at the back of the group to make sure they can keep up with our walking pace.

I stop the group halfway along Stonegate and explain, 'So, everyone has heard of Guy Fawkes, who tried to blow up the Houses of Parliament, haven't they? Well, he was born in one of these houses in 1570. His father, Edward was a church lawyer and a prominent protestant in the city, but he died when Guy was only eight years old. His mother remarried a catholic and they moved to Knaresborough.'

There's a lamp post beside me so I unravel a poster and secure it with blue tack. The two women read the details and I explain what we'll be doing at the author event.

One of the women says, 'Aww, that's a shame we leave York tomorrow but good luck with it all.'

Everyone nods and I point out Guy Fawkes Inn. 'So, the ghost story here in this pub is that one night a woman saw a black-hooded manly figure skulking in a corridor but as she stepped bravely towards him, he disappeared through a door!'

I shrug my shoulders. 'Believe that if you wish.'

We continue and reach the outside of the minster where I turn to everyone as they gather around me in a circle. This is one of the things I like about being a tour leader. I'm surrounded by a crowd of people who look at me to help and instruct them. It's the one area of my life where I'm in complete control. I am the boss and their leader. Note to oneself, remember this when you get up onto the stage at the author event it'll give you a boost.

Older men might say I should be in command at home but when I think of Barbie, I know this isn't true. To use an up-to-date phrase, we share responsibility and manage our lives together at home. But to use an older phrase, I know who wears the trousers in our relationship, and it's not me. However, I grin, she does look great in a tight pair of jeans, so, who's to argue, certainly not me because I'm more than happy to take the back seat.

I speak up loudly now to make sure everyone can hear. 'Well, here we are outside our glorious York Minster. I know many of you will have been inside during your visit to our city, so I'm not going to bore you all with facts. You've probably read it all in the pamphlets, but I am going to tell you a little ghost story.'

I can see everyone lean in towards me and I lower my voice trying to make it sound creepy. 'In the 1820s tours of the minster were conducted, and two sisters decided to join in. During their tour, a tall man wearing a naval uniform approached the sisters, whispered into one of their ears and then incredibly disappeared into thin air before their eyes!'

I hear the older lady at the back of the circle gasp. I know I've got them with me, so I continue. 'One of the sisters recognised the man as being their brother, who had died while serving in the Navy. Rumour has it this sister had made a pact with her brother while they were both alive. They agreed whoever was first to pass away would return to the other living sibling and give definitive proof there was an afterlife.'

The older man pulled the peak of his cap further down over his forehead as though he was saluting the sailor. 'I was in the navy myself but not in the 1820s of course!'

The other men in the group nod in respect and I grin at the old man. 'Thank you for that, Sir, and where did you serve?'

He told us it had been in Portsmouth during the second world war and a general buzz went around the group.

I say, 'So, do we think this woman received some pretty compelling proof from her brother that he is still around and floating in and out of the minster?'

A louder discussion takes place with the men dispelling ideas of an afterlife and a naval ghost in the minster. However, I can see the scepticism in their faces as though they aren't one hundred percent sure.

I raise my voice again. 'And now we are off to The Golden Fleece Inn, which was built in the early 16th century and claims to be the most haunted public house in York!'

The women ooh and ahh while holding their husband's arms and we set off again along the street. This time I purposively walk alongside the older couple and chat to him about his naval career. Not because I'm particularly interested, but because we have a couple of busier roads to cross, and I want to make sure they're safe.

I smile, and say to the group, 'Now, look out for the alleged twenty-three cat statues guarding the walls and rooftops in York. Let's call out as we go and hopefully no one will spot all of them because if you do the saying has it that you'll be cursed for the rest of your life!'

The group laugh and I walk everyone across to The Shambles. On the side wall of the first shop, I stick up another poster. I steer everyone around in a circle back to Stonegate to the last stop on the trail, Ye Olde Starre Inn. As we walk, I ask, 'Can anyone navigate the labyrinth of snickelways in York?'

The group shake their heads and I smile. 'Well, neither can I but I did look up the word snickelways and this is the definition. They are alleys, ginnels, snickets and lanes, many of them ancient which run between the streets in York,' I say. 'They are often hidden, requiring some effort to discover. And, boy, oh, boy is he right. I've never been able to fathom them out and I have lived here for years now.'

We stand in a snickelway near the inn and as I'm speaking, I notice a couple at the end who are standing looking at each other. I can tell by their gestures they've met before. Words are exchanged but I'm too far away to hear, however, I instantly recognise the long white trousers which make Margaret Smithson's legs seem endless. I see the two-toned glasses and know I'm not mistaken – it's definitely her.

She throws her arms around the man's neck and buries her face into his shoulder. He pulls her into him and wraps his arms around her waist. It's a very close embrace not just a friendly hug and I can tell this isn't the first time they've been in this position. She is used to fitting into his body.

The man who is hugging her has his back to me so I can't see his face, but one thing I do know is that it's not Geoff. This man is short and stocky with reddish brown hair. He also looks much younger than Margaret - a toy boy, I wonder?

Instantly, I turn the group around back out onto the main path. I take a deep breath and let it out slowly. I don't want Margaret to see me and think I'm snooping on her. That would be turning the tables on what she'd previously asked me to do. Shaking what I've seen out of my mind, I concentrate on the tour.

A few customers pass me to go inside the Ye Olde Starre Inn, and I hand them one of our event leaflets and then the bartender comes outside. He agrees to hand out more leaflets inside and put up a poster. I know most of the staff who work in the pubs and restaurants, and we have an unspoken rule. They're willing to do things for me because when I stop the tour outside their pub, customers very often return to eat and drink. It's a case of you scratch my back and I'll scratch yours.

I call the tour to an official end. 'So, I do hope you've enjoyed our walk around the city tonight. Are there any more questions or anything I can help you with?'

Some people tell me how much they've enjoyed the tour which makes me feel happy especially when I receive a big round of applause. I give a long theatrical bow and one by one they come up to me shaking my hand and pressing notes into my palm. I love the subtle English way of tipping appreciation, and tonight I pocket seventy pounds which is going straight into the wedding day fund.

Wandering home, I'm now left with the quandary of what to do about Margaret. Do I tell Goeff, or not? I'd want to know if Barbie was cheating on me, but would I appreciate being told by a new boss. If Simon, a very close friend took me aside and confidentially told me what he'd seen, I would appreciate the news coming from him. However, my relationship with Geoff is totally different. And, of course, I've already found out from Rodger that Margaret is a complex character.

I sigh, on the other hand, Geoff could know Margaret is having a dalliance with another man. And if I tell him what I've seen it could be mega embarrassing. Not only for me, but him as well.

I've already made a fool of myself with Geoff once and don't want to repeat this mistake.

Turning onto Victor Street, I decide to do nothing at the moment and wait until I find the right time and place to tell Geoff, if at all.

Chapter Twenty Two

With my trusty old holdall, I'm standing outside Simon's house on Kings Road. Finally, which after what seems like months of waiting, but it's not, we are going to the world-famous Theakston Crime Writing Festival today. And I'll be meeting with the publishers tomorrow.

Barbie has dropped me off before heading up to Durham to visit her mam. She seems to think it's a done-deal with the publishers and last night gave me a celebratory night in bed to congratulate me on something which hasn't actually happened yet. Was I going to argue - you bet your life, I wasn't. I smile wishing I'd the confidence in myself that she has.

I yawn feeling tired after a late night writing the plot for my new book. I've already decided to set the new mystery in Harrogate where I'm surrounded by the golden-age detective, Agatha Christie. And hopefully some of her success will rub off on me. Although it will be set in modern times, this old spa town will make a great setting for my twists and turns in a whodunnit story. I've three to four red herrings plotted to throw readers off the scent and plan to use a psychological twist at the end.

June opens the front door and greets me warmly. 'Hi, Clive, come in and I'll take you up to your room,' she says. 'Simon is out buying wine – he reckons you'll definitely be celebrating this weekend.'

Oh, God, here is someone else who thinks I'm going to walk away with a contract, but what if I don't and disappoint everyone? I'll feel foolish if I don't make the grade. It's almost like being back at school again and a

shiver runs up my back. I step inside the hall, she plants
a kiss on my cheek and then mounts the first stair.

I follow her upstairs while she chats about the weather
and how excited Simon is for the festival. I agree with
her all the way onto the landing when she turns into the
first room on the left and walks inside. 'The bathroom is
the next door which will be all yours because we have an
en-suite in our bedroom.'

'Hey, that's great,' I say, and drop my holdall onto the
carpet.

At the sound of their landline ringing, June hurries back
downstairs and calls, 'Come down when you're ready,
Clive and we'll have a coffee.'

The perfect host, I think and look around the big room.
Already at ten in the morning, the sun is streaming
through the large window. I walk up to the beautiful
white wood shutters and flip them to keep out the glare.
The décor is light grey, and everything matches perfectly
with white wood furniture and a sleigh bed. I plonk
down onto the edge and give a little bounce. Good
mattress, I think, and punch up the soft pillows. Yep, it's
going to be good staying here rather than travelling back
and forth every day.

I couldn't afford the festivals weekend package which
does include a hotel for three nights. However, I know
this is a good offer for people travelling to Yorkshire
who don't know the area. The cost provides everything
for their stay.

I pull the zip along and open my holdall. Barbie has
helped me pack and as usual has thought of things I'll
need which I hadn't. I lift out my toilet bag and find a
tube of sunscreen remembering her words, 'It's forecast

to be hot and sunny,' she'd said. 'You don't want to greet the publishers with a red shiny forehead!'

I chortle. She knows me so well which makes me wonder, how do women think of these things? She's right of course, I think lifting out my blue dress shirt and cream chinos.

She'd also said, 'I know you've got jeans and vests for the other days, but you can't meet the publishers without looking nicely dressed – it'll make the wrong impression.'

After hanging these up and placing my underwear in a drawer, I loop the strap of my laptop carry-case onto my shoulder and head back down to June.

I can see she's out in the back garden sitting on a hammock swinging herself backwards and forwards as she chats on the phone. Her legs look so cute in white shorts and a matching T-Shirt. I can't help thinking she looks like a little girl herself. It's a narrow long garden and would be perfect to bring up a family.

As I wander through the hall I pass by Simon's study. From the doorway, it looks as messy as mine at home, and it's a relief to see another writer is just the same. After decorating, June reckoned it was called, a friendly man cave.

Simon had sighed and said to me, 'Whatever that's supposed to mean?'

I'd shrugged, 'Hell, do I know! Barbie calls our lounge, Modern Urban Farmhouse, as if I should know what she's on about. I just nod - it's simply the lounge to me.'

I smile at the memories, continue through to the kitchen and then outside to June. Simon had once told me they can't have children. All he'd told me was that June had done IVF but felt so poorly, he wouldn't let her do it again. I hadn't asked anymore. I figured if he wanted me to know more then he would tell me. Perhaps that's a man thing, I think and shrug. I do feel empathy for people, but struggle to express it sometimes like many other men, and this occasion had been one of them.

When Simon returns, and after coffee, we walk the short distance up to The Old Swan Hotel.

***

The Crime Writers Festival takes place each year and first started in 2003. It's got bigger and gone from strength to strength over the years and now takes over the whole town for four days. People travel here from the around the UK and from all over world to enjoy the festival.

We walk up to Swan Lane through the gardens and small park area. The flower displays are full of colour and look beautiful. They do the town justice and add to its oldie-world charm. I mention, the Floral Summer of Celebration, and huge pink shoe near the train station.

Simon nods. 'Yeah, the gardeners have done a fantastic job this year,' he says. 'And June tells me the community volunteers have organised summer holiday activities for the children with pop-up parties in the parks and free cycling sessions.'

I smile. 'Hey, that's great. They also do an amazing job with food banks supplying parcels of basic provisions or even cooked meals. It's something I'd like to get involved with, but it's finding the time now I've taken on another job.'

He nods. 'June is thinking of helping with the service who look out for our neighbours to prevent loneliness, not that we've got many elderly people on our street,' he says. 'But it's a worthwhile cause.'

Remembering the posters, I point out the Pump Room Museum to Simon. 'I've never been inside the museum, but I love the old Yorkshire stone and round shape which looks great with the art décor black and gold adjoined building.'

Simo nods, 'I have, June took us to an art exhibition inside once and it's every bit as spectacular inside as out. And, the old sulphur springs are still in the basement where people used to come to take the waters – it stinks!'

I grin as we reach the hotel and Simon lifts out his leaflet, saying, 'The website states, no matter the weather, the world's hottest celebration of crime writing swings into town. It's the friendliest Festival with its feet firmly on Yorkshire ground. Hang out with your heroes, get an exclusive insight into the Next Big Thing, rub shoulders with the UK's leading agents, editors and publishers. Be inspired and join in the drama at Agatha Christie's old haunt: the luxurious Old Swan Hotel. It would be a crime to miss it!'

'And it certainly would,' I say, to which he grins.

We stand outside the hotel admiring the sight before us. I whistle through my teeth in awe at how they've transformed the old hotel to accommodate the amount of people who attend. It's a big hotel in old grey brick which has four floors of windows - the top floor being smaller attic windows. To the right on the ground floor is the wide hotel entrance with a couple of steps or ramp. The frontage to the left is covered in ivy which only adds to the grandeur of the building with extensive well-kept gardens and lawns.

The emblem of Theakston's Old Peculiar Ale has a black background with a red circle and is all over the building. Two billowing flags are at the car park entrance and deck chairs with their printed logo are scattered around the lawns in between two big white marquees.

I say to Simon, 'Oooh, it all looks fab, doesn't it?'

I know Simon doesn't easily show his emotions but can tell by the way he is grasping his day-pass, and his eyes are gleaming that he is as excited as I am. We present our tickets and head inside the hotel.

The hallway is as impressive, if not more so, than the outside. Polished wood floors gleam. The high ceilings with white covings and hand rails on cream painted walls do justice to the splendid old building. Large chandeliers strategically placed down the long hallway glisten.

I grin. 'What a perfect setting to imagine mysterious stories and plots.'

Simon pulls me by the arm across to a big glass showcase on the wall. It shows the front page from The Daily Sketch in 1926 with a photograph of missing, Agatha Christie. In capital letters it says, 'MRS AGATHA CHRISTIE FOUND ALIVE.'

Simon says, 'And here is the first lady of mystery and suspense.'

We both stand and read the newspaper article and talk about her books. I wonder if Agatha had any deathbed confessions to investigate? I remember reading, The Pale Horse novel and how a deathbed confession was admitted when an old priest was murdered.

Smiling, I wonder if the master sleuth would have found out if Jake did drown his sister before he confessed? And, would Agatha have investigated the twin mix up and discovered Neil's identity crisis. I nod to myself, yep, Agatha would have been one step ahead of me and Geoff, long before the culprits confessed.

Further along the hallway is the large conference room. For the festival this has been turned into Waterstones book room and we hurry inside to see large shelves full of crime, mystery, and thriller novels from all the famous authors here for the weekend. They've set aside an adjacent room where book-signing is taking place. I whisper to Simon, 'Oh, look, there's Anne Cleeves and Mark Billingham!'

It feels like we're kids looking in a sweetie shop window not knowing what to look at next or which to choose.

'Let's look through these later,' Simon says. 'The first author panel is starting soon.'

I nod. 'It's certainly a great place to write. I feel energised already and it hasn't even started yet.'

We back-track outside and wander up the side path to a gigantic white marquee where one of the special guests, Val McDermid is about to start. Inside there are hundreds of red chairs all in rows with a small black stage at the front. White silk billowing drapes cover the ceiling making it look like a ginormous tent with two lengths of camera lights down the centre beam.

Already, the first ten rows in front of the stage are full. I say, 'Simon, we're going to have to get here quicker for the other sessions if we want a good view.'

He nods and we sit on the aisle seats. Val enters the marquee with the interviewer, and they take their seats. Val explains how she'd wrote her latest book in lockdown, and they discuss the pandemic, the effects this had on everyone, and how people talked about their own funerals and what they would want. It was a scary time and many people looked to the past for safety and security which resulted in a splurge of old crafting and upcycling because people know this works.

The points are thrown open for a question session and I'm mesmerised. I can't think of another word to describe how I feel listening to Val and her memoirs. I glance at Simon who is furiously scribbling notes in a small notebook and figure maybe I should be doing the same, but I'm transfixed.

The next session is from a group of authors who discuss the importance of location and sense of place in crime novels. Paula Hawkins, who wrote, "Girl on the Train" is mentioned and how she wrote her story around the daily commute on trains into London.

I can't help thinking of Jack the train driver in Durham. Although, he would never have driven a South West train because he worked for LNER, but is it true that train drivers look into the same windows and patio doors every day? Are they fascinated by seeing the same people and sequence of events in homes they travel past. And, do they notice when things are amiss and make up stories about people's lives like Paula had done. In fact, this could be the way Jack met his lady friends in towns on his rail route up and down the North East mainline.

The hour has flown by and after thunderous rounds of applause we leave the marquee amongst a buzz of how great the session had been. Heading back down the track we sit on the grass in the sun enthusing over what we've just seen and heard.

Simon collects us coffee and we're joined by some of his book club friends. They're a friendly bunch and we talk about books, books, and more books. I'm in my element and enjoying every second. There's a discussion about the Nordic authors, in particular, Jo Nesbo and how popular they are on TV.

Simon laughs, 'And to think it all started with Sarah Lund's Faroese jumper!'

Someone mentions the time and we all scramble up to head back for the next session with debut authors. We get seats nearer the front this time and I pick out the notebook from my jacket pocket. I whisper to Simon, 'We might get some tips here for our library author event?'

'Yeah,' he says, and smiles wistfully. 'I wonder if either of us will ever get onto a debut panel like this?'

I nod. 'Well, I think you could with your latest novel – it's brilliant.'

I receive one of his shy smiles and take a moment to reflect on our friendship which I feel has grown so much in the last few months. We get along easily now and there are never any awkward silences, only a comfortable atmosphere and appreciation for our mutual love of writing.

The panel begins and I scribble notes about the type of questions to ask. How to draw the author out and talk about what is important to them in their work. Where their ideas come from and what they'd like to write in the future. I learn how crime writers are notoriously known for being friendly and I wonder if writing about people makes them more approachable.

I smile, or maybe it's because writing is a solitary job, so when they get into a social setting, they let their hair down. We certainly see this tonight at the dinner and quiz, where the authors are the life and soul of the party.

Chapter Twenty Three

It's lunch time on the last day of the festival, and I'm pacing around the high-back chairs in the lounge waiting for the editor from the publishing house to arrive. I reckon it's the best possible atmosphere to talk about my work. I feel energized with a mix of nerves but excitement too. I can't wait to meet with her. Thankfully, there aren't many people around as most have gone into the dining room to queue for the buffet lunch. I sit down and stroke the soft red velour chair which feels comforting somehow and matches the long drapes at the windows.

If I'm successful, it'll be a massive step up to being a full-time author from writing as a hobby in between my day jobs, and if I follow in Simon's footsteps, it will take a lot of courage. Simon is convinced he will succeed, but I bite my lip unsure if I can be just as brave. Of course, he is financially in a different situation, and although Barbie makes a good wage, it would be a lot of pressure to put on her if I did the same.

At the sound of my name, I look up to see a middle aged lady in a green flowery dress. I jump up, cursing myself for letting my mind wander. She holds out her hand and introduces herself as the editor.

We both sit back down, and she reaches into her handbag pulling out a piece of paper which I can see is a copy of the email. I'm asked to tell her about myself as she sits back in the chair and crosses her legs.

Sweat forms between my shoulder blades in the dress shirt I am wearing. However, I'm pleased I made the right choice because she is neat and tidily dressed. My super-hero T-Shirt would have given entirely the wrong impression, although I love it because Mrs Webster gave it to me last Christmas.

I've already rehearsed a little speech and launch into my talk about the two novels I self-published on Amazon.

She looks over her black framed glasses and smiles. 'Well, Clive, I loved your book, Death in the Caravan Park, and we'd like to take it, and you, onto our author list.'

My insides surge with happiness. I'm cock-a-hoop but try to control myself although I feel like dancing on the tables. 'T…Thank you so much - that's fantastic news!'

She smiles. 'Your characters in the caravans are brilliant. I felt as though I was peeking through the windows at them. You've ticked diversity boxes very well, and suspense is threaded through the story from start to finish – well done!'

I grin. 'Well, I actually went to stay at Whitley Bay holiday park to get the vibes,' I say. 'I'd never had a caravan holiday so reckoned it was a good way to discover the seafront, lighthouse, and causeway. And, basically, that was me sitting writing on the veranda every day - it flowed so much easier.'

She actually claps her hands together. 'Marvellous strategy, Clive, so what's next?'

I tell her about the novel I'm starting which will be set here in Harrogate and after I read the pitch, her eyes light up. I can tell by her fluttery hands that she's enthusiastic. The paper on her knee slides to the carpet and I bend over to pick it up.

Taking it from me, she leans forward. 'Right, in fact, let's make this a two-book deal, Clive,' she says. 'If you can give me some more great characters in this next plot, it'll be another good one.'

I'm dumbstruck for words, which is a first for me. My mouth dries and my stomach is tumbling. All I can manage to do is nod and keep muttering my thanks. I'm astounded they've offered to take me on board, and with the proposal of another two books.

'So, we'll be in touch with contracts to sign next week via email and deadline dates for edits and publishing day,' she says. 'Now, if you'll excuse me, I'm meeting some friends for lunch.'

I stand up when she does. I shake her hand again and feel like bowing as though she's our old Queen, but then I figure, she is like royalty to me.

When she leaves the room, I plonk back down in the chair and feel tears prick my eyes. I've done it, I want to cry. I've actually got what I dreamt about for the last three years. Finally, it's all come together. This editor obviously believes in me and I'm going to be a published author.

I shake my head still in disbelief and want to hear Barbie's voice. I pull out my mobile and call her. I feel quite emotional and when she answers, I tell her my news. She promptly bursts into the tears I'm struggling to hold back. With many congratulations and kisses blown down the phone, she says, 'I'll see you later tonight – now go tell Simon!'

I run outside onto the lawn and scan the area for him. I look behind to see him sitting cross-legged on the grass in a shaded corner. I literally run over towards him, and he looks up.

I feel like I've won the lottery and let go of all my pent-up emotion. I do a cartwheel across the grass towards him, and he throws back his head to howl in laughter. Two female writers are sitting nearby in stripey deck chairs. We'd talked to them yesterday and found out they are from Gateshead Scribblers Writing Group.

One of the ladies calls out, 'Hey, Clive, are you drunk already?'

I wave and plop down next to Simon and tell him my news. I'm starving as I gabble the whole conversation out to him. He's already bought us sandwiches and cokes which I devour as though I haven't eaten for a month.

Lying back on the grass with my legs outstretched and my hands clasped behind my head I look up at the blue sky. I'm filled with an overwhelming happiness and am longing to see Barbie tonight.

'Come on, Clive,' Simon says, interrupting my time-out. 'The last panel is about to start.'

We head alongside others back up to the big marquee for the last time to hear a session which has been called, The Chortling Experts. I reckon it's a strange name for a subject which is bound to be gloomy with a police procedural advisor, a world-renowned forensic anthropologist, a mortician, and a psychologist who provides training for the police force. The leaflet tells me they are all authors in their own specialised fields. I take my seat next to Simon but don't think I'll be able to concentrate on the subject which sounds quite depressing. However, once it starts it is anything but.

They give examples of their writing works and make fun of themselves in humorous situations with sights, sounds, and smells. I whip out my notebook to record the details because they're so interesting.

The police advisor explains how the public have a level of understanding nowadays with watching TV shows and expect the police force to do the same. The public think the police will have all of the equipment and DNA results asap, whereas in real life, it takes two to three weeks for results which means people get angry.

I can see Simon nodding in agreement. I pay particular attention to the psychologist who explains about psychosis. The signs and characteristics of this mental disorder, and the more she explains about their low emotional status, with no empathy but charming and manipulative personalities, the more I think about Michael, and if he is a case to study.

Afterwards, we head back to Simon's house, and I collect my holdall. My head is buzzing with information overload and my brilliant news. I simply want to be at home with Barbie relaxing and meditating. I feel quite lightheaded with life itself and wonder, is this what everyone calls the feelgood factor?

While I'm sitting on the train back to York, I receive a message from Geoff. 'Michael has rung and asked if you would write the version of his dad's confession into a story for a newspaper so he can get the £10K. I've told him, no, that is something you won't get involved with.'

Chapter Twenty Four

*Michael sighed. It was three days now since he'd
stormed out of the meeting at work with his line manager
- it hadn't gone the way he thought it would. The guy
had been, as far as Michael could see, a wise-ass smarty
pants.*

*The manager had believed the snivelling porter who'd
made the complaint even though Michael had accused
him of intimidation. Michael lied and told the manager
how the other porter had laughed at him because he
couldn't complete his log sheet. But still the manager
hadn't taken his side and told Michael it was a
prerequisite of the job. If he couldn't complete the
sheets, then his position would need to be re-considered.
He'd been given something called, a verbal warning.*

*Michael had scraped the chair back, and shouted,
'You're out to get me, and laughing at me as well!'
Then he'd stormed out of the room.*

*Once home, he'd lied to Sherrie stating he had been
given another week's holiday because he worked extra
shifts during the year. She had raised her eyebrow in
doubt, and he had seen the smirk on her face. She soon
begged for forgiveness when he'd dragged her into the
bedroom and all his misdemeanours were forgotten.*

*Last night in bed he'd had the weirdest dreams, in fact
they turned into full blown-out nightmares. Even when
he woke, Michael could still hear the voices from the
dream shouting and laughing at him. He tried to
convince himself that they were just dreams, but they'd
seemed so real, it was uncanny and scary.*

*Sherrie had got up, dressed, and stood over him with
her hands on her hips. 'There's an awful smell in the bed*

- you'll have to get in the shower today, Michael,' she'd cooed.

It was a pathetic sounding voice that she thought was caring and loving. But all it did was irritate him.

He'd sprang out of bed and raised his arm above her head yelling, 'Get out and leave me alone!'

And she had. She'd grabbed her phone and handbag then ran out of the apartment. He sighed now, he hadn't hit her – or had he? Michael shook his head not being able to remember. His thoughts had been, and still were, very confused.

His mobile laid on top of the bookcase and began to ring, he glanced at the screen. It seemed to be vivid changing colours from red to green to purple. He rubbed his eyes and wondered if he was seeing things? His vision cleared and he saw the call was from the manager. He ignored it as he had done the previous calls in the last two days. This time, he couldn't be bothered to listen to the manager's grovelling message, 'Please come back and talk to me.'

Michael stared at Clive and Simon's books on his shelves. Startled, he felt someone was behind him. Was it Sherrie coming to apologise and beg to be taken back? He swivelled around but when he looked behind there was no one there. The room and apartment were empty.

Clive's books were signed of course, but he planned to ask Simon to do the same after the library event. Michael gritted his teeth. He held the clicker switch in his hand from the newly installed light. He flicked it on and off at intervals watching the books light up and then fade.

Life was so unfair, he wailed. How did they get to be so clever to write a book? It's what he would love to do, if only he had the brains. Clive told him his childhood had been crap with dreadful parents and he'd ended up in an offenders' institution. So, Clive hadn't been born with a silver spoon in his mouth either. However, Simon had been to York University and done a journalism course or had he got that mixed up and it was the other way around?

Michael remembered how Geoff had said, 'No, Clive wouldn't be able to write his story for the newspapers, it was something they wouldn't get involved with.'

He snarled, who did they think they were turning down his commission? It maddened him, as though his money wasn't as good as anyone else's. He knew that being writers, Clive and Simon could make the story sound scandalous and exciting. Michael was sure the newspaper would print it and give him £10K. Of course, he would give the authors a little money for doing it – he wasn't that mean.

His pot of money would get him and Sherrie out of this small apartment and into a nice house. He planned to ask Sherrie to marry him soon and he wanted to have the best house on offer. That way, he wouldn't be beholden to her parents with rent, which he hated.

Michael frowned, perhaps he could get Simon to write the story if Clive wasn't allowed? To be honest, he thought Simon was a better writer than Clive. He enjoyed Simon's books much more as they were manly and ruthless. There was more danger and murderous crime while Clive's books seemed to be intrigue and mystery. Michael knew this fitted into what was called, the cosy crime genre. But who wanted cosy?

He certainly didn't – he wanted blood and guts like any other crime reader would.

Michael looked around the bedroom especially at his beloved bookcase and the sabre hanging above which had been a gift from Sherrie's aunt. She'd found the sabre in a charity shop, but Michael thought it was hideous.

Sherrie wasn't keen on it either, but loved her aunt, so up it went. He lifted the sabre down and slipped his long fingers through the gold ridged handle which was a snug fit. He ran his finger along the curved edge. It was certainly sharp enough, he thought, but Michael was sure it won't come to that.

The room was large for what was called by estate agents, a guest bedroom and because it was on the end of the block it had two small windows and two traditional column radiators. The grey carpet was nice, although a little rough to sit on for any length of time but would do well enough for the scheme he had in mind after the event.

Michael planned to ask Clive and Simon back to the apartment for a drink and he'd get Sherrie to make a few snacks. This would crack two birds with one stone and when he had them together, he'd ask Simon to sign his book and write the newspaper story.

Tiredness swept over him, and he lay flat staring at the ceiling. It didn't look white now but orange and yellow with some red mixed in which he knew were flames. Maybe he could join their writing group and learn how to write his own stories. He knew exactly what he would write – it would be all about fires.

There were lots of causes for fires, faulty wiring, dirty chimneys, careless smokers, a lightning strike, and in their case at home, flammable liquids. But there were also forest fires. Michael could only dream about these and how he'd love to see a big forest ablaze. And, the final cause which had been his favourite past time, a child playing with matches.

He cast his mind back to the night of the fire, and how he'd loved the flames. It had been sad to think of his mam upstairs, but it had been a spectacular sight.

Since being a little boy, he'd loved fire and flames. The colours and height. The strength and force. The howling noise. He could list his favourite bonfires every 5th November from being eight years old. The huge one at Gateshead, Saltwell Park. Exhibition Park, in Newcastle, otherwise known as The Town Moor. And Whitley Bay, although this one had been tame compared to the others.

Most children of his age had been content to run around with sparklers, but he loved to be close. Too close sometimes and was often pulled back by well-meaning adults which had annoyed him. His own parents never pulled him away. He could have walked through flames and his mam and dad wouldn't have even noticed. Michael wondered if anyone would notice now.

Chapter Twenty Five

'I don't mind admitting I'm a tad anxious, Simon,' I say. We are sitting in the library conference room with minutes to go for the start of our author event. Well, I should say Simon is sitting, I'm pacing around the chairs.

'Sit down and breathe,' Simon says. 'You're like a panther prowling about the place.'

I plonk down next to him and chortle. 'There's a story somewhere in that sentence?'

He nods but doesn't laugh. I can tell he's nervous too by the way he wipes his sweaty palms down his corduroy trousers and twists his watch around his wrist.

Simon has already told me June wasn't coming because she's got a busy day in the Turkish Baths with fifteen ladies on a hen party having spa treatments, champagne and high-tea.

Cynthia is flapping around everyone chatting like the proverbial hostess. She's donned her best silver turban with drop pearl earrings, necklace, and bracelet for the occasion along with a blue and silver kaftan. The big windows are open because already at midday, it's hot and sunny. The sun streams through the windows and glistens on her silver making it a sight to behold, if you like that type of thing. I don't think Barbie would agree with Cynthia's choice of bright pink lipstick, but our leader is in her element.

In fact, we've all dressed for the occasion apart from Simon who I know feels comfortable in his usual clothes and I can't blame him. We've enough to feel uncomfortable about speaking in front of an audience without scratching at stiff necklines, although I have worn my white shirt and chinos.

Fen has her snacks laid on the table with a white cloth at the back of the room. She's pouring drinks for everyone of different flavoured fruit squash in small white plastic cups. There'd been an issue earlier because Cynthia had brought her crystal-cut glasses to the library carried by Darren, who is actually stronger than he looks. However, the librarian argued about the washing up of glasses afterwards even though Fen had insisted she would stay behind to make sure it was all cleared away.

Fen is wearing a long red silk dress with a high collar and cloth buttons which looks stunning as the dress swishes around her dainty feet. Where other men don't tend to notice these things, I do, but mainly to use as descriptions when I'm writing.

There's a general buzz in the room as people chatter and sip their drinks. I smile noticing how Darren has his plate piled with snacks and is now showing people in the front row his photographs of trains. They look bored but I can tell he's determined to persevere. He's ditched his scruffy anorak, thank goodness, and is wearing a T-shirt with, yes wait for it, an old steam train on the front which he's obviously bought from the museum.

He'd once told me, 'If I can get just one person interested in visiting the railway museum then I'll feel as if I've done a good job for the day.'

I look over towards Fen and see Angela with her in the wheelchair although she does looks better. Her eyes are bright and smiling again, emphasised by the blue blouse she's wearing. As each person collects their plate and snacks, Angela hands them a serviette. I suppose to an able-bodied person this seems nothing, but to Angela, it makes her feel as though she is contributing albeit in a small way.

I hear and see Fen pointing to the posters surrounding the stage. 'Angela's clever son made all of these,' she says.

I watch Angela preen. And rightly so - she's very proud of him. I'm sure Cynthia has sent him a bottle of wine and chocolates as a thank you from us all.

Cynthia approaches us and we jump up from our seats. She hugs Simon first and then wraps her arms around my waist and hugs me tight. She whispers, 'Break a leg!'

I know this is what they say in the theatre on opening nights and in her youth, she'll probably have had many of these well-wishes.

'Now,' she says. 'The authors are ready back stage and I'm sure both my boys will do a great job – so off you go.'

Cynthia stands in front of the first row of chairs and claps her hands. 'Attention everyone, it's time to start our little event,' she calls loudly in her shrill voice. 'Allow me to introduce you all to two of our writing group who are going to interview our special guests today.'

There's a general noise of anticipation around the room as people settle themselves comfortably in the seats. We both take to the stage and receive a round of applause from the audience. I pick up the microphone from the table. My stomach is in knots and my top lip is sweating. I try to remember how confident I feel when doing my historical tours in York and telling my stories, although there's more people here than the small tour groups. I can only hope this audience will take kindly to us.

Pulling my shoulders back, I take a huge deep breath in, look to the back of the room, and let it out slowly. 'Hello, everyone,' I say. 'I'm Clive Thompson, and this is my partner in crime, Simon Travis.'

My little pun receives a titter from the ladies especially. I can see everyone smiling back and willing us to do well. My voice sounds a little rough on the microphone, but I figure it's the same for everyone. It's like recording your voice onto the old telephone answering machines.

I'd noticed stepping onto the stage how one of the middle chairs in the front row was empty. On the chair is a spare leaflet which puzzles me because this was my guest place, but now I see Michael crouch along the row and slide into the chair in an effort not to disturb people. I look at him and nod. I'm so pleased he's made it because I know he'll enjoy the talk. It looks like he's showered although I can't smell him from the stage, but he does look fresher somehow and is wearing his nice clothes.

We've written the introduction between but as Simon lost the toss he speaks out, 'Hello everyone, so by way of an introduction, I've written a few words about Harrogate.'

I smile at him and nod. My heart is thumping, but I know this is what we both need going forward, it'll help to promote our books with the publishers. And it's good practise for us in case we ever get to the dizzy heights of book signing at the Crime Writers Festival.

Simon continues, 'I've lived in Harrogate all my life on Kings Road. I worked as a solicitor in the sale of houses section for years, therefore, to use an old saying, I know the town like the back of my hand,' he says. 'I read on Google that if there's a choice between York and Harrogate, the latter is always the best option which might upset my crime partner here because he lives in York!'

I clutch my chest and give a comical look of outrage which makes everyone laugh. I can see Cynthia nodding in delight from her front row seat. Young Darren is sitting next to her and has his hands on both cheeks as if he's feeling our anxiety.

'Harrogate is often referred to as a spa town in North Yorkshire and as a true Yorkshireman I can honestly call it, God's Own Country,' Simon says, and waits for the audience who nod and smile in agreement. 'Harrogate dates back to the 16th century and was known as, 'The English Spa' in the Georgian era. An area to the north of the developing town was set aside for residential buildings to provide entertainment for the increasing numbers of visitors. The Georgian Theatre, hospital, and royal pump room were soon opened, and the town grew in popularity with its quaint streets, historic houses, and landscaped gardens.'

I see Simon's shoulders slump in obvious relief and know it's my turn again.

'So,' I say. 'Without further ado, it's my great pleasure to introduce, Sally Moor, and Ricard Gwent to the stage. Please give them a good old Yorkshire welcome!'

Everyone claps loudly as Sally and Richard walk onto the stage and take their seats. I sit opposite Sally, and Simon opposite Richard.

'Hello to you both and thanks for coming,' I say. 'I think I can speak for everyone here when I say we're thrilled to have you visit us.'

I reckon Sally is around early forties and has huge eyes with long lashes. She has an enormous smile with big lips painted in bright red lipstick.

'Thanks, Clive,' she says, and smiles at the audience. I can feel her warmth radiating from that big smile and I'm sure everyone else can too.

'It's great to be invited here from Birmingham to talk about my book which by the way, is set in the Caribbean.'

I sit forward and ask, 'Is that where you were born?'

She nods. 'Yes, we came here when I was two, so I look on England as my home, but I've loved finding out about the homeland, and of course writing about it. As a Caribbean woman it was an honour and a pleasure to revisit old family traditions.'

I smile. 'It's strange because the first book I wrote was set in London where I've never been before, but I set my second novel here in the North East at Whitley Bay and it was so much easier to write.'

A discussion begins between the four of us about the importance of settings in our stories and that's it. My shoulders are down, I completely relaxed and am engrossed talking to Sally about her ancestors which are characters in her book.

My anxiety, as they say, has left the building. I can tell Simon is likewise when after two more questions and answers with Sally, he jokingly intervenes and brings Richard into the conversation.

Although twenty-five year old, Richard looks straight-faced with a long beaky nose and brown framed glasses. He has a brilliant sense of humour and bounces off quips with Simon which have the audience in hoots of laughter.

Richard tells the story of his novel set in Aberdeen. 'Yeah,' he says. 'I know I'm a bit of a comedian but feel I have to be to lighten the gruesome, deadly stuff I write about!'

There's a vigorous discussion between Simon and Richard about finding the humour and sentiment in tragedy and death.

Sally says, 'That's mainly because the part of our brain we use to imagine and tell stories is in the emotional side of our mind.'

Richard agrees. 'You're right - some of my crime writing friends strive to see the comical side of their murderous characters,' he says. 'But one of the funniest men I've ever met is the well-known author, Peter James.'

Simon nods. 'Now, some of his books are gruesome!'

The conversation carries on until I look out into the audience and see Cynthia tap on the face of her watch. I know she's telling me it's time for questions and answers. I'm almost sorry to end the discussion because I've enjoyed it so much. To think it was something I'd been dreading through nervous anxiety.

I comically prize the microphone from Simon and say, 'So, everyone, we are running out of time which is a great shame because I know Simon and I could talk to our guests all afternoon, but we do want to give the audience a chance to ask questions.'

Simon grins. 'Hold up your hand up if you've a question for Sally or Richard, or both together?'

We'd already agreed I would do the running around with the only mobile microphone for two reasons. One, I'm a little slimmer and more agile than Simon, and two, he did the introduction.

I see a hand shoot up in the second row and head off clutching the microphone. I recognise the postmaster who is Scottish, and he asks Richard about Aberdeen. Happy with his answer, I gallop off to the back row and hand the microphone to a lady who I'm sure works in the old pump room museum. She asks Sally about the township in the Caribbean because she's been there on holiday.

I hurry back to the front row and see Michael's face beaming at me.

'Hello, Clive,' he whispers.

I nod and smile at him then pass by Cynthia who swipes her fingers across her throat. Another theatrical gesture, I think and know we are to close the session. Hoping back up onto the stage, I say, 'So, everyone, all there's left to do is thank our guests once again for coming. And if you want to buy their latest books, Sally and Richard will sign your copy at the table in the corner.'

I bow with a flourish and help Simon to manoeuvre Sally and Richard from the stage to begin signing their books.

Simon and I are surrounded by Angela, Fen, Darren, and of course, Cynthia who is gushing to say the least.

She cries, 'Darlings, you were fabulous! Now come along everyone – there's Champagne back at my house.'

I receive a hug from Fen and Angela as does Simon. Darren claps both our shoulders exclaiming in his squeaky voice, 'Ooohh, well done to both of you – you were simply marvellous!'

My cheeks are flushed, and I can tell Simon struggles as much as I do to accept compliments. However, my insides soar with happiness. I have to admit I'm relieved we did so well and didn't let ourselves, the audience, or the writing group down.

I feel a gentle tap on my other shoulder and swing around to see Michael. When I'd seen him from the stage my earlier impression of freshness is quashed, because if anything, his smell is worse, and I take a step back from him. His clothes are not freshly ironed, although I must admit he's made an effort. I wonder if he's still off work and why Sherrie has not taken him in hand over his hygiene and clothes.

He stands with his hands in his pockets staring down at the carpet, and mutters, 'Clive, I…I just wondered if you and Simon would like to come over to the apartment for a quick drink?'

I'm aghast and my mind whirls struggling to think of an excuse. 'Oh, Michael, we are all going to Cynthia's to have a little celebration,' I say. 'Could we make it another day perhaps?'

Michael looks almost tearful, and I feel Simon behind me. I introduce them and Michael goes into raptures about his books especially his last novel. 'I…I don't want to be a nuisance, but would you sign it for me, please?'

I can see Simon melting at Michael's pathetic stance, much as I did when I first met him.

I had told Simon about a man's sad case that I've been working on, his horrendous upbringing and then his father's confession. Of course, I hadn't named the man and know Simon would never utter a word about the case, on that I'm a hundred percent certain.

Michael glances up at us both with such a lost puppy-dog look on his face that although neither of us want to go, I know Simon is just as kind-hearted and can tell by the droop in his shoulders he's going to relent.

Michael almost whispers. 'It would only take a few minutes. I just live across the road?'

Simon smiles. 'Yeah, of course, we'll pop in for a few minutes, won't we, Clive?'

I grin and squeeze Michael's shoulder. 'Yeah, we'll come along now for five minutes then return to help clear up and go to Cynthia's.'

I find Cynthia in the corner of the room chatting with Richard and Sally. Draping my arm along her shoulder, I say, 'We are just popping over to a friend's flat to sign his books – we'll only be five minutes because he lives on Raglan Street, see you soon.'

Cynthia nods and waves us off.

***

Geoff has left a message on my works mobile and as we head up the stairs, I read it quickly. 'Sherrie has left Michael and is at her parents – she's asked me to bill her there. Apparently, Michael is behaving very strangely. Sherrie was scared of him. He's become unbalanced because he's stopped taking his medication, which according to her, keeps him on the straight and narrow. So, I'd be careful if I was you.'

I shrug knowing this makes sense now. Sherrie isn't home to keep Michael on the right track, mainly to shower, I think and wrinkle my nose. However, we'll only be there a matter of five minutes which isn't long enough to get embroiled in any of his issues.

We follow Michael out of the library and out into the warm sunshine. Michael crosses quickly over the road more or less in front of a car, but Simon and I hang back a little to let it pass by us. This gives me time to whisper to Simon, 'Ten minutes – tops. I just feel that sorry for him.'

Simon nods in understanding and we catch up with Michael at the steps to the apartment block.

Simon says, 'Ah, I remember when this block of flats was converted and updated.'

I wait for Michael to reprimand him for calling them flats but he doesn't. He opens the main front door and holds it open until all three of us are in the hallway.

'Gorgeous old floor tiles,' Simon comments.

I watch Michael's shoulders lift. 'Yes,' he says. 'We love living here.'

He selects his key for number one and opens the door. We follow him inside. I'm expecting drinks in the lounge which is where I've been before. And basically, that's the last thing I remember clearly because suddenly I feel a crack on the back of my head and hear an almighty thud then everything goes black.

Chapter Twenty Six

I can hear Simon's voice shouting. 'Clive! Clive! Are you okay, Clive!'

I see stars when I try to open my eyes and blink rapidly. There's a taste of blood on my lip and know I must have bitten it. My vision clears and the first thing I see is that I'm lying on a grey carpet. It feels rough and I want to close my eyes again then head back off to wherever I've been, but Simon calls my name again.

'Simon?' I moan, and groggily lift my head up from the carpet.

'It's okay, mate,' he whispers. 'Try and sit up a bit more and you'll be able to see me.'

I twist my shoulder, but it hurts, and I grimace in pain. I lift my head further up and stare across the room. Simon is sitting with his back to the wall with both his arms across his chest. His wrists are tied to the long pipe on a column radiator.

I cry, 'What the!'

'It's Michael – he's gone crazy,' he whispers. 'He hit you over the head with something and when I jumped across to help you, he pushed me over. I landed in a heap then hit my head on the skirting board. I was pretty dazed but felt him drag and tie me up to this radiator. I was too stunned to struggle.'

'Oh, my God!' I cry and look further around the room. 'W…where is he?'

'I don't know,' Simon says. 'He practically danced out of the door a few minutes ago when you were still knocked out.'

'But why? I mean, what does he want? What's he going to do and why would he do this to us?'

Simon doesn't comment but shakes his head slowly. 'Not sure, but I'm not arguing with him,' he says. 'And I tell you something else, he might look like a small weakling, but he must have some bloody strength to drag me across the floor, but he did.'

I take a deep breath and know I have to help my friend. It's my fault we've gotten into this ludicrous situation. I give myself a little shake to clear my head and think straight, but it hurts.

Simon says, 'Try and sit up, it's better than lying flat.'

It's only now that I realise, Michael has tied me to the second radiator in the opposite corner to Simon. I feel the thick twisted rope cutting into my skin and wince. Without putting too much pressure on my wrists, I carefully wriggle and manoeuvre myself up into a sitting position then sit cross-legged with my back against the wall.

The room swims a little but then settles and my focus returns. I breathe out slowly with thunderous pain in the back of my head. The room feels airless. I feel stifled and sweat soaks through the collar of my shirt. I want to pull it away from my neck but groan because I can't reach.

I look at Simon and feel tears prick the back of my eyes. He has an egg-shaped bump on his forehead and a trickle of blood on his cheek. My good friend isn't equipped to deal with anything like this. I sigh, and neither am I. We might write about these situations but it's a different matter when someone does this to us.

'Don't worry,' I say, feeling no conviction whatsoever but know I must be positive for his sake. 'I'll figure something out.'

I see Simon suppress a smile. 'And how in God's name are you going to get us out of this unholy mess?'

I shrug. 'I haven't figured that out yet, but I will, Simon. I'm not going down without a fight!'

My heart almost skips a beat when Michael prances back into the room and stands in front of me with his hands on his hips. I follow Michael's glance over his shoulder towards the door and swallow hard. Was someone else in the flat? Did he have an accomplice? Was someone out there pulling his strings? Was it Sherrie, and have I been completely taken in by her as well?

Michael cackles loudly. 'Ah, it works every time, it's the element of surprise, you see, just like Sherlock Holmes.'

I don't answer. He steps closer to me and pulls the rope even tighter around my wrists. 'You're not going anywhere, Clive,' he says, and scurries out of the room again.

I look across at Simon. 'Eh? What on earth is he up to?'

Simon shrugs. 'I don't think I want to know, Clive.'

I peer up to the window at the grey venetian blinds. The window is open a little but not enough to let much cool air into the room.

'Is your window open, Simon?' I ask, and he nods.

The room is empty other than us two and that infernal bookcase on the other side. I look over towards the door which is not fully closed. The rope is tied so tightly there's no way I'd be able to loosen it. I figure our chances of escaping from here are non-existent. Therefore, we'll have to be rescued. I think back over the last hour and remember telling Cynthia where we were going. However, she was in her lady of the manor performance, so she might not remember.

On the book case I see novels from all the famous crime writers, Harlan Coben, Stephen King, and James Pattinson. I nod to Simon and grudgingly say, 'Well, at least we're in good company on the book shelves.'

Michael returns and when he nears me, I cower away from him further up against the wall. Partly out of fear, but also because of the stench – it turns my gut. His breath is revolting with food remnants in his teeth which makes me wonder when was the last time he'd brushed them?

Michael's eyes dart around the room now while I look at him properly for the first time today. His neatly trimmed beard is much longer, and he scratches it whilst pacing. How had I not seen that wild look in his bloodshot eyes in the library? I shrug, perhaps they weren't like that a few hours ago.

'Well, it's lovely to have house guests for a while,' he says, pacing slower in circles. His voice has lowered and menacingly he continues, 'Of course, it would have been nice to have you both here voluntarily, but if this is the only way I can get to you, then so be it. And that bloody boss of yours! Who does he think he is telling me you can't write my story!'

Michael starts to pace in opposite directions now. I feel quite dizzy watching him. He mimics a gruff manly voice who I imagine to be Geoff's, and says, 'The PI said it's not something we get involved with.'

I sigh in understanding now and wonder if it's worth trying to talk to him out of this situation?

I decide it's worth a shot. 'Michael, doing this to us isn't going to get your story written.'

'Oh yes, it is,' he yells. 'You're a couple of bloody morons!'

His ugly voice startles me, and I feel my heartbeat thrash in my ears. I squeeze my eyes tight shut and pray when I open them again this will all be a bad dream. But it doesn't happen. It's real and it's happening to us.

I strain to hear his words as he rambles incoherent thoughts to himself. The realisation begins to sink into my befuddled mind. Michael looks totally unbalanced, deranged, or whatever the correct word is to use.

Silently, I curse. I should never have helped him by signing my bloody books. None of this would have happened if I hadn't felt sorry for him and walked away like Geoff always does to avoid getting involved.

Barbie has always said that I'm a soft touch and how I shouldn't concern myself with people I don't know. The thought of her makes me choke back a sob. I've left my watch at home on the desk and have no idea of the time but wonder if she'll be home yet.

Michael stops pacing and stares at me intently. His eyes don't seem to blink often enough which makes him look even more weird, if that's possible.

I try again. 'Michael, I can't apologise enough that Geoff wouldn't let me write your story, but if you untie me, I'll make some calls. I can find another writer to do it, there are people called ghost writers who do this type of thing.'

'I know what they're called,' he snaps back. 'I'm not an idiot!'

Mine and Simon's mobiles are ringing over and over again. I know it'll be Cynthia or one of the others wondering where we are. They won't want to start the celebrations without their two top stars, and I sigh.

My own phone is in my back pocket, but it's opposite to where my hands are tied and no matter which way I turn, it's out of reach. I grind my back teeth and clench my jaw. How dare he? How dare he put me and Simon in this situation and upset our lives just because his is a mess.

I hang my head and take a slow deep breath to try and remain calm. I can smell sweat from my own armpits now and grimace. When I shuffle my backside, I feel the work mobile Geoff gave me which is smaller and in the side pocket of my chinos. It feels loose enough and may slide out. I think of Geoff's message when leaving the library. He'd told me to be careful, but who could have thought Michael capable of this? Not me, but I so wish I'd taken more notice of Geoff's warning.

I give Simon a purposeful raise of my eyebrows and wink at him trying to convey I have a plan. Simon can see I'm up to something and keeps Michael talking about his book in an effort to divert him.

I remember at the crime writers festival how other authors commented upon using mobile phones and how they're such a powerful tool in writing. They were like carrying a mini computer around and nowadays it's possible to find out anything on a mobile especially in social media.

Michael lifts Simon's book from the case and walks over to him then reads out a passage in a pathetic whining voice.

'I can feel the hard mattress dig into my back but can't move a muscle because he has tied my wrists and ankles to the bed. I'm spread-eagled and I'm terrified. What is he going to do to me? He stinks of beer and is a huge man with menacingly cold eyes. It was the first thing I'd noticed when he sat opposite to me in the pub. His cold stark eyes, as though there was nothing behind them. Dead-pan eyes, I've heard them called. There'd been a sheet covering my body through the night but now he stands to the side of the bed and whips it away. I'm left shivering with cold and humiliation. 'Aaah,' he grins and licks his thin mean lips. 'What do we have here?'

Michael has his back to me, and I start to wriggle my backside around praying the phone will slide out, and bingo, it does just that. My hands are tied right up onto the radiator pipe, but I roll and lift my knee up then flop down onto the phone as hard as I can. All I can hope is that I've pressed number one to alert Geoff I'm in trouble. And boy, am I in trouble. I have never needed him as much as I do right now. Even if number one hasn't registered, I hope the GPS tracking system might just kick-in. I shrug at Simon as if to say let's hope for the best.

While manoeuvring myself, I'd listened to Michael's reading and thought how the dialogue would make a great film or TV drama. I tut and shake the ridiculous thoughts out of my mind. I often think of silly things when under pressure.

However, it's never occurred to me before when writing horrible scenes how readers might copy them. What we write is pure fiction. And I know, as any other level-headed reader does, that Simon's novel, Abducted, is a fabricated story. Even though the stories we write are as true to life as possible, I've never given a thought to the effects our words have on a reader.

Maybe some readers take the words and resemble them to happenings in their own lives? Had Michael done just that? Had he been held against his will at some stage in his life? Or I think, feeling a shiver run down my spine, had Michael held a woman against her will like in Simon's scene?

Michael leaves the room again slowly looking deep in thought. My stomach flips. What's he going to do? So far, it's only been aggressive words shouted at us with an unreasonable demand, but are there more dangerous things to come?

I murmur to Simon about the GPS on my work phone from Geoff and what number one means. 'I don't know if it's going to work but thought it worth a shot.'

Simon whispers, 'At this stage anything is worth trying. Now I know how it feels to be held against your will. To feel powerless. To have no control. To be scared, Clive, and be lost in your own thoughts all the time.'

I try a half-hearted smile. 'Well, I've done research about some mental health disorders which I used for a character in my book, Death at the Caravan Park, and how distinct personalities were great for crime writing. Of course, I'm not a doctor, but unless I'm very much mistaken, Michael is showing major signs of paranoia. Well, at least the signs I've read about.'

Quietly, I tell Simon about his background and explain how Michael wants to copy his dad by selling his own story to a newspaper. 'Geoff wouldn't allow me to do it, not that I'd want to of course,' I say. 'However, I would agree to anything now just to get my hands free because I know I could overpower him.'

I can hear Michael pacing backwards and forwards outside the door in the passage. His thoughts are obviously in a terrible upheaval, and I wonder if I could manage to calm him down.

'Michael,' I say quietly. 'I can see what you went through in the fire years ago was horrendous and it's understandable that it's come back to haunt you – but maybe we could get you some help?'

Michael pokes his head around the door and stares at me. He shakes his head slowly from side to side. It's not a vehement shake as earlier, but more of a mollifying gesture. Am I getting through to him, I wonder?

I push on, 'I mean now-a-days, these counsellors can do amazing things, so someone might be able to help you?'

I see his shoulders slump. Is he wavering and softening towards my suggestions? But he disappears again, and I sigh.

I try to rationalise our plight and whisper to Simon, 'Well, so far, we've been lured to this flat under false pretences by a deranged man. We are tied to radiators and can't move, but there is no sign of a weapon, as yet. Therefore, apart from being held against our will, all we have to deal with is Michael who appears to be obsessed about having his story written by one of us. Unless he has other ulterior motives, I wonder if it's possible to talk our way out of the situation. I can tell by his temperament that arguing or antagonising isn't going to help.'

Simon agrees. I look over to him and my chin trembles. It's all my fault he's going through this because I brought him into the flat which seems even worse after our great success in the library. Not, of course, that being held against your will would be a pleasant experience at any time, but it's a painful anti-climax. We should be at Cynthia's right now sipping Champagne and celebrating with our friends.

'Simon, I'm so dreadfully sorry that I brought you here,' I say. 'Please believe that I had no idea Michael was this crazy!'

Simon shrugs his shoulders. 'There's no need for apologies, Clive, of course you weren't to know.'

Deep down in another way, I'm selfishly glad I'm not on my own to face this madman because, I sigh heavily, that's what Michael has become.

Chapter Twenty Seven

In comparison to creeping away quietly before, Michael now bounces back into the room. His mood swings seem to be from one extreme to another. He pulls at his long fingers as he had done the first time, I met him. And sporadically cracks his knuckles standing in front of me.

His face reminds me of the posters up at Belsay Hall in Northumberland which are scattered throughout the gardens. We'd taken Mrs Webster there for the day last year. English Heritage are renovating the old hall and putting on a new roof. There's an image of a man's huge rugged face and dishevelled hair amongst tree trunks. It reads, 'Belsay Hall where the legendary wild man of Belsay roams.'

I reckon Michael is this wild man swinging violently from quiet introvert to crazy extrovert.

'So,' he demands. 'You're both staying here until one of you agrees to write my story!'

I shake my head. 'Em, we've just had this conversation, Michael.'

He rushes across to his bookcase and pulls down the sabre from the wall bracket. He yells, 'Did you hear what I said? I want that £10K!'

I jump and can see out of the corner of my eye, Simon visibly shrinking further down the wall. He looks as scared as I do.

My mouth dries and I lick over the crusted dry blood on my lip. I start to hyperventilate, and my heart is pounding. All my muscles tense and I can't feel the rope on my skin anymore, in fact, I feel nothing at all in my limbs.

'L…Look,' I say. 'Just take the rope off and we'll sit and talk this through? Either of us will gladly write your story for you, if you'll just let us go and then I'll help you anyway I can.'

He begins to pace. 'I need the money to get out of this place and buy a house for me and Sherrie,' he wails. 'Her parents hate me too, and I don't want to take their money for rent because my dad owes me big time!'

While he's shouting and raging, I keep my eye on the sabre. A slight ray of sunshine from under the blind glistens off the length of the blade which looks lethal. Michael's fist is gripped in the gilt ridged handle. He curses aloud and then spins on his heel and marches out again.

I take in a deep breath and feel my heart stop pounding. My breathing returns to normal. I glance across to the open door, but all I can see is the same grey carpet and cream walls. There's an old mothball smell wafting around – a little like sweaty socks which wasn't here when I visited before. Obviously, the place was missing Sherrie's cleaning touch.

'Phew!' I sigh. 'That was a close one.'

Simon nods. 'I know, that blade is scary!' he says. 'I was looking at those books on his shelves and thinking of Stephen King and Peter James's novels, and the horrific things they do to people with knives!'

'Aww, Simon, you know as well as I do, they're made up by stupid authors like us who've nothing better to do with their days than scare readers.'

He shrugs his shoulders. 'Yeah, but he's already recited a scene from my book – what if he tries to replicate one of their scenes with that sabre?'

I try to smile. 'Let's cross our fingers he's not rationale enough to think of that.'

I've lost all sense of time and look up and under the blind. The sun is still shining but doesn't seem as bright, so I figure it must be early evening. I notice Simon is wearing his watch. 'What time is it?'

He swivels his wrist to look at his watch. 'It's nearly five now - we've been here two hours,' he says. 'I think it's been the longest two hours of my life.'

I nod and uncross my legs because they're cramping. Stretching them out straight, I relax my tense shoulders and creak my neck from side to side to ease the ache.

I mumble, 'Dear, God, how much longer are we going to be here, and more to the point, what's he going to do to us?'

A tear leaks out of the corner of my eye as I wonder if I'll ever see and hold my lovely Barbie again. Will we get out of here alive? I gulp but shake my head defiantly. We have to and we will. I lower my head to my hands and wipe the tear away with my thumb. I must stay positive for Simon's sake if not my own.

Simon mutters, 'When he came up close, I smelt the cigarette smoke hanging around him. And you know, although I gave up smoking years ago when we did IVF, right now, I'd willingly sell my soul for a drag on a cigarette!'

I nod. 'I've never smoked,' I say. 'But as usual weird things come to mind when I'm stressed and I've just remembered an author friend whose catchphrase is, 'Roots & Reasons. In which he means that everyone has a family history and background. I reckon it's the memories from the night of the fire which has flipped Michael over the edge.'

My stomach growls and my throat feels as dry as the desert. I tell Simon this and he nods his head.

He mutters, 'Yeah, and I need the loo.'

I nod. 'Me too.'

Simon wriggles around and I know he's uncomfortable.

'Clive,' he says. 'I'm probably feeling a tad over-emotional at the moment which considering the pickle we find ourselves in is understandable, but if I don't make it out of here and you do, please tell June how much I love her. And I couldn't care less if we never have a family. She's always been, and still is, more than enough for me.'

I catch a sob in my throat at this big shy guy waxing lyrical, as they say, and shake my head. I don't want to listen to his negative thoughts because I have to remain positive. I recall the author talk this afternoon about finding humour out of tragedy. I say, 'Well, the same goes from you to Barbie. And with my life insurance money tell her to ditch that godawful bright red kitchen!'

Simon laughs out loud, and I chortle. That's better, I think knowing I've got to keep us going and stay strong. 'But to answer your request, Simon. No, I won't tell June because I know you'll be telling her yourself when we get out of here – which we will – it's only a matter of time before they come looking for us,' I say and smile. 'And, my friend, if you pee your pants in the meantime – your secret's safe with me.'

Chapter Twenty Eight

Michael is like a caged animal – he's pacing the room again clutching the sabre in his hand. His face is white, and his eyes are red-rimmed. I wonder if he's been crying? He's obviously suffering some type of psychotic episode and I question his level of sanity. Is he completely insane? It looks like his thoughts and emotions are so impaired he has lost contact with reality, as in, me and Simon. I wonder if it would help to talk about something or someone he cares about.

I think of his girlfriend. 'Michael, what's happened to Sherrie - did you have a falling out?'

He spins around to me, and I nod knowing I've at least got some type of reaction. There's a small light behind his eyes and I can tell he's thinking about her.

'Yeah, we did, and she ran off. She left me like everyone else does. But she'll be back and will get what's coming to her,' he grimaces. 'You see, it's easy to play on her because Sherrie hates being alone. All I have to do to get what I want is use this fear and control her in the bedroom. That's where I make her wear all the tarty make-up to look like a hooker I've just paid for.'

I don't answer, but think of Sherrie, the beautiful young girl who I like, it makes me shudder. God knows what she has put up with living with him. I remember her love and concern for Michael and grit my back teeth. He's not even grateful to have her in his life. Sherrie is just another person for him to manipulate and connive against. Slowly, I shake my head and feel my toes curl.

I sigh listening to the slight hum drum noise of traffic outside. Normal everyday life is going on, and no one knows we are here suffering in this ludicrous situation.

People are leaving work from the offices on Raglan Street. They're so close, yet in another way, so far because they know nothing of our torment. Shoppers will be returning home with bags of food and treats to prepare evening meals. Children will be running around freely through the parks having being released from the school gates. And the librarian across the road from where we sit will be closing up for the day.

Stupidly, I wonder if the group cleared away properly in the library after our author session. I think of them altogether in Cynthia's home tipsy now on Champagne and celebrating without us. Their two golden stars are missing and sitting in purgatory with a madman – who would have thought it?

And then, as if an angel drops down from the sky, I hear Cynthia's imposing voice. 'But it has to be along here somewhere because Clive said the flats on Raglan Street!'

I shake my head in disbelief at what I've heard. Maybe I'm following in Michael's footsteps and losing my mind too. A smile creeps around my lips, but I need to know I'm not imaging it. I cry, 'Oh, Simon, can you hear what I can hear?'

Simon shuffles up further from where he'd slumped. He lift's his shoulders, smiles for the first time since we found ourselves in this mess, and whispers, 'It's Cynthia!'

I want to cry at the sound of her voice which I've always held dear while she's reading her prose. I close my eyes and pray that one day we'll be back in the library at the writing group doing exercise prompts.

It seems like a world away. But, I sigh, a lovely world all the same.

I listen carefully, and then hear Darren's squeaky voice saying, 'Ah, but like I said before, they could just be in a pub somewhere getting pissed.'

'No, Darren,' she says. 'Simon might, but not my Clive, he doesn't like drinking. And I know he'd never let me down like this. If he said he would come, then something serious has happened to stop him from doing so.'

They're just outside our windows. I recognise Fen's gentle murmurings and wonder if Angela is there too. It would be great if her hubby was with her because he's a big man. Although there's nothing he could do to help us from outside. I hear them putting clues together to try and find us. It brings a lump to my throat that they care so much and have come looking.

I take a deep breath and try again to reason with Michael. However, I know rational judgement like I used in the caravan last year with the German misfit, isn't going to work with Michael. This is a different situation altogether. Michael is not listening to me but is mumbling to himself. His hair is standing up on end and his eyes are glazed over altogether now.

Amongst other words I hear him say are, 'That line manager thinks he's in charge at work but he's not! I am!' He stops pacing and starts to make marching steps with his feet - he's taken off his shoes and his feet are bare. 'I'm in charge of these two idiots tied up and I'm the boss. I know what I'm going to do, and they don't!'

I sigh and try to ignore his delusions of grandiose which sounds like a petulant child. Maybe it's because I know our friends are outside that I want to do something positive. Something to help ourselves get out of this crazy mess. But what?

Once again, I try to think of a way out. If Michael came close enough to my feet, maybe I could trip him up then wrap my legs around his body. But then what? It's not as if I can pounce on him when he's down on the carpet. I wouldn't be able to secure him because I can't move my arms or hands.

I listen again and hear Darren outside saying, 'But there's three levels of windows, Cynthia, how do we work out which ones they're in? And, they might not even be in there.'

'Press all of the buzzers, sweetie,' Cynthia urges.

I can vaguely hear the soft buzz of buttons but it's so distant I reckon Darren has started on the top floor. Of course, they don't know we are on the ground floor. And, that we are being held against our will. They might think we are ignoring them and leave us here in the flat?

I whisper this to Simon who agrees. 'I know, I thought of that, too. The last thing we need is for them to move away.'

Michael is in the corner alcove and seems to be staring into space where actually it's a blank wall he is facing. Maybe he can see things on the wall we can't see. Is he hallucinating, I wonder? I know a delusion is hard to dismiss if you have an unshakable belief in something.

Simon is nearest to the corner window and suddenly, he shouts at the top of his voice, 'We're in here, Cynthia! We're being held hostage on the ground floor!'

This startles Michael and he rushes over to Simon and gives him a sharp dig in the shoulder with the handle of the sabre. Simon cries out in shock and obvious pain.

My blood boils and I jerk my head. 'Stop it! Don't hurt him!' I yell. 'He's done nothing to you. He came here to do something nice and sign your books – you ungrateful sod!'

Michael cackles and begins to pace in circles once more. Simon has obviously rattled him into action again. I remember how psychotics have no empathy or feelings for other people. He doesn't care about me or Simon. He doesn't care about anybody but himself. It's futile and I can only pray we aren't going to be hacked to death by this madman with his sabre.

I ask Simon, 'Hey, are you okay – has he hurt your shoulder?'

Simon sighs. 'It's fine. It was worth it just to get their attention outside, so they know we are actually in here.'

Then we both hear Cynthia shout, 'We'll get you out, Clive – don't worry, darlings!'

Simon nods in approval and says, 'Even if they don't get to us in time, it's great just to know they're out there and rooting for us, and we aren't alone anymore.'

I nod and repeat Simon's sentence to myself. We aren't alone anymore. I blot out Michael's ramblings in my ears and strain to catch every single sound from the other side of the windows.

There's a dog barking somewhere off in the distance and what sounds like a big lorry passing by on the road. And then in the quiet, almost eerie atmosphere, I'm sure I can hear Barbie's voice too. She's making the little noise in her throat when she cries. Unless, of course, it's wishful thinking on my behalf and it's not her.

Perhaps, she's rang June or the library wondering where I am because I haven't told her I'm going to be late. The earlier calls and messages that pinged onto my mobile would have been from her. I've always let her know where I am especially when she's at home and not away on a contract. As I like to know where she is, and then neither of us worry about each other.

It's a well-known fact when people behave out of character there's something wrong and Barbie knows this. I swallow hard hating the fact she's worried and doesn't know what's happening. Or in this case, maybe not knowing is a blessing.

And then my whole insides surge with relief and happiness. Heat radiates through my chest, and I grin recognising another voice – it's Geoff.

The GPS must have worked. I imagine him strutting about trying to get the upshot of what's happening. I don't have to strain to hear his words asking key questions. Have you rang the police? How long have they been in there? Is Michael on his own in the flat? Is he armed?

Cynthia answers him loudly in her dramatic stage voice. I can imagine her sizing Geoff up to see if he fits her perception of Clark Kent's "Superman" figure. I sigh and relax my shoulders a little. It feels like the SAS has arrived and I know if anyone can get to us in time, it'll be Geoff. I whisper, 'They're coming to get us, Simon.'

Chapter Twenty Nine

Michael runs out of the room and pulls the door shut behind him. It hasn't been secured fully on the catch and opens ever so slightly with the breeze from our windows. The door is open enough for me to hear that he's in the kitchen area of the lounge. He's put his trainers back on and I can hear them squeak on the floor tiles.

Michael is chuntering about a great bonfire at Saltwell Park in Gateshead when he was a boy. How the flames had been amazingly tall, and the colours had blown his mind. There's a clanking of a tin and the noise of cupboards opening and being slammed shut. I try to imagine what he's doing, and decide sardonically, he's not making us a cup of tea.

I've always had a good sense of smell. I can inhale the closed containers of Indian take-a-ways and tell Barbie which is her dish with coconut before she peels back the lids. I can smell different flowers in the garden and name them. And when Mrs Webster comes to our house, I know she's in a room before she enters because of the Channel No:5 she wears. We buy her a bottle each year for Christmas.

So, even though I'm across the small hallway from the kitchen area, I inhale the unmistakable smell of petrol. I gulp and feel the hairs on the back of my neck stand to attention.

Looking over to Simon, I can tell he hasn't noticed and is concentrating upon what's going on outside the windows in the street. I say nothing, not wanting to alarm him and figure there's time for that later, if need be.

It sounds as though Michael is emptying petrol from a container into something else because I hear the stream of a liquid. I recall his statement from a few weeks ago, and how his father had used an old lawnmower filled with petrol when he started their fire.

My mind races. Oh, my, God, is he going to do the same here? Is he repeating everything that happened to him years ago? Does he intend to set the flat alight? My previously relaxed shoulders hunch up to my neck and I wriggle upright against the wall. I'm on red alert and my stomach churns when I hear what sounds suspiciously like a match being struck.

I want to blubber. Is this how it's going to end? Are me and Simon going to burn to death in a fire?

We both smell the smoke at the same time, and I look at Simon.

He whispers, 'We've had it now…'

I shout, 'No! They'll get us out - I just know they will!'

I sigh wishing I felt the same conviction inside myself that I've used in my voice.

Suddenly, I hear Darren shout, 'There's smoke at the other window on the ground floor!'

And then there's a lot of different sounds. I can hear loud words shouted. 'Fire! Fire!' and, 'Dear God!' and, 'We've got to get them out!'

There is noise coming from inside the building now because someone has activated the fire alarms. The shrill alarm bell blasts in my ears and if my hands were free, I would cover them. Neighbours from upstairs come running down the stairs shouting. A baby is crying. Children and women are screaming.

I hear the main front door opening and slamming shut as they all run outside. I say a little prayer, hoping everyone has escaped. If me, Simon, and Michael aren't going to survive this fire, I'd hate to think other innocents have perished too.

People must be outside from the offices around the block of flats and reckon they'll be standing with our friends.

Angela yells, 'Look! There are flames at the kitchen window!'

Darren shouts, 'There's an outside tap – everyone get into a chain with buckets, or anything else you can find!'

I hear the clanking of what seems like metal containers and a woman shouts, 'Will a kettle do?'

'Oh, God, they're trying to douse out the flames through the kitchen window,' I shout to Simon.

Darren yells to someone. 'Have you got a fire extinguisher in your office?'

'Yes, yes, I'll fetch it!'

Geoff shouts, 'Clive, is the fire in the room where you are?'

I yell back, 'Nooo, it's in the kitchen!'

'Look, I'm going to try and open the window wider – so shield your face!'

No!' I shout seeing Simon start to cough. 'Do Simon's window first on the corner – he's nearer the fire!'

Simon isn't. I am the nearest but out of the two of us, I need it to be him that survives. He's the innocent party in this bloody farce. There's no point telling Simon to shield his face because our hands are tied, but I say, 'Look away from the window and bow your head.'

I watch one of Geoff's stubby nicotine stained fingers unhook the catch on Simon's window and open it wider. With his arms outstretched and with his large fists he reaches up and rips the blind down.

Michael runs back into our room and howls like an animal.

Temper rages inside me knowing I can't help us, or our rescuers, because of this bloody rope. I pull at the rope around my wrists although all I'm doing is scraping my skin. I yell, 'Arrrgh!'

The rush of cooler air sweeps into the room and I breath it in deeply. Geoff knows like I do if he opens the windows and lets air into the room of the fire it'll ignite the flames even more.

I see Geoff at my window unhooking the catch and doing the same. He yells, 'Are you okay?'

I shout back, 'Yeah, but the smoke is on Simon's chest – get him out first!'

'Okay,' he yells. 'The police are battering the lock on the flat door – won't be long now!'

Simon has his head bent as far down as he can to where his wrists are tied and has managed to pull the sleeve of his old brown sweater over his nose and mouth. Thank God, he's wearing that, I think knowing we have to get him out soon.

I can see Simons shoulders' shaking as he coughs into the sleeve. I feel the acrid taste in my mouth and start to cough too. I know in minutes the flames will be in this room and feel panic rise in my chest.

I look at Michael who is standing with his back to us watching the flames in the hallway. He looks mesmerised and in some type of trance.

His face is childlike, and he turns to me muttering, 'Ooohh, look at the colours – see how high they are!'

Michael!' I scream 'Untie us for God's Sake!' Then I start to plead, 'Pleeease….'

But he ignores me, and I know he's too far gone and out of it. Michael is in another place altogether. He's not here in this room and I realise all hope has gone to save him from himself.

Then we all hear the sirens.

The smoke makes it dark in the room and I can't see Simon now but keep talking to him. 'You'll be okay – they're nearly here now – just hold on!'

Simon grunts. I'm hoping his voice is just muffled because the jumper is over his face.

Within seconds Geoff charges into the room from the main bedroom door like a raging bull. He's followed by two firefighters tramping inside wearing all their gear.

Michael scarpers away from them before Geoff can reach him and virtually walks into the flames. He lifts the sabre up into the air.

'NOOO,' I shout. 'Don't!'

A big smile spreads across his face when he roars, 'Dad didn't start the fire on his own – we did it together!'

I howl as Michael plunges the sabre into his own chest.

Chapter Thirty

Simon is coughing and heaving with the smoke. I can hear and see more firefighters in the hall with hoses tackling the flames on their way to the kitchen.

A firefighter cuts the rope from Simon's wrists and places an oxygen mask over his face then two of them carry him out of the room.

The firefighters shout, 'This way – come with us!'

Geoff cuts the rope from my wrists and helps me to stand up. My feet feel numb, and my legs shake – they feel like jelly. I stagger with the help of Geoff on one side and another firefighter on the other.

'You, okay?' Geoff asks looking down at me. Sweat is standing on his forehead and concern is etched in his face.

'Y…Yeah, I think so – just get me outside into the fresh air.'

We hurry through the main bedroom and out into the bottom area of the hall which has been doused by the firefighters. Within seconds we are out of the front door and into the mayhem on the street where I hear a loud clapping noise.

***

I gulp at the fresh air and take huge lungful's into my chest. I rub at my wrists and see a female paramedic put another oxygen mask over Simon's face. They carefully strap him into a stretcher-chair and put a blanket around his shoulders.

I hurry to him and put my hand on his arm giving it a squeeze. 'A…Are you okay?'

Simon looks up at me with a black face and red-rimmed eyes. From under the blanket, he takes my hand and squeezes it back. 'Yeah, I will be.'

I'm carefully moved aside by the paramedics as they wheel him towards the emergency ambulance parked up on the kerb.

I look around at the chaos in the street. It's only six o'clock but the sky looks grey or is it remnants of the smoke. Police cars are at either end of the street blocking the traffic. Two fire engines are parked up with their lights flashing. Firefighters are zipping about at the back of the engines unrolling hoses and pulling on their huge beige jackets with yellow fluorescent stripes.

The ambulance with Simon inside is parked up on the right hand side kerb and a second ambulance is at the top of the street. I glance back at the flat with the door propped open and think of Michael lying in there amongst the flames and smoke.

I wonder if the second ambulance is for his body? I shudder. Bile rises up in the back of my throat. Putting my hands on my knees I lean over by the ornate railings at the bottom of the steps and retch.

Another paramedic comes to me. 'How's your chest – can you breathe properly?'

I nod and take deep breaths. 'Yeah, just a bit sickly, but thank you, I'm okay.'

The police have a cordon of blue and white tape around the pavement to the flats. People are holding up their mobile phones taking photos and filming the scene from behind the tape. If I wasn't gasping and trying to clear my throat, I'd scream at them to stop. It's macabre and our suffering is nothing to remember with any relish.

I recognise Cynthia's gold turban where she is standing with her arms around June on one side and Barbie on the other. A police officer lifts up the tape. Barbie and June duck underneath and race towards us. June rushes to the ambulance and I see her climb into the back while Barbie literally throws herself at me.

I wrap my arms around her waist and bury my head in her shoulder. Tears pour out of me unchecked. Not manly, I know, but I can't stop them.

She holds me tight and rubs my back. 'You're safe now, darling,' she murmurs, over and over again.

It's beginning to dawn upon me that yes, I am. We got out, and yes, I'm safe. Or should I say, all of these people got us out. They've saved my life and I know tears aren't far away again. My knees start knocking together and my whole body begins to tremble.

'I have to sit down,' I mumble.

I see Geoff sitting on the top step of the next office block. I lift my head from Barbie's neck and with her holding tightly onto my hand, I stagger over to him.

I sit down on the step next to him and ease my shaky legs out. Barbie stands behind with her hand on my shoulder.

I don't speak to Geoff. I don't know how to start thanking him for saving my life. I simply put my hand on his knee and squeeze it hard.

He nods. His face is white with a black streak down the side of his cheek. He runs a hand through his thick hair. 'Jeez! That was a close call,' he murmurs, and glances at me with a sideways look. 'You, okay?'

I feel bad for him. If I was sitting in his place, I would feel responsible in some way because I work for him.

Although I know this is ridiculous because it's happened out of work hours, and I hadn't gone to see Michael as part of our investigations. It had purely been a social visit to sign a book. And none of us knew how deranged Michael had become.

I repeat the sentence to myself, humour in the face of tragedy and nod. 'It was scarier than being up on that roof!'

His big shoulders shake a little and I see his lips twist into a smirk at my wit. He lifts his head up and looks at me full on now. 'But seriously, Clive, had you no idea how crazy he was when you went in there?'

I shake my head and let out a long slow breath. I'm not sure at this stage how much I want Barbie to know. We don't keep secrets and I'll probably tell her every minute detail later, but it might spook her now and I figure she's been through enough in the last hour.

I look up to her, and ask, 'Barbie, will you go over to see June and find out how Simon is doing, please?'

She smiles. 'Yes, of course, you stay right there. I'll be back.'

Obviously, Geoff has figured out my diversion tactic and nods. 'Neatly done,' he says. 'She sounded a bit like Arnie Schwarzenegger saying, I'll be back.'

I snigger at the reference but launch into the full blown account of what happened from leaving the library when Michael seemed calm and his normal pathetic self, to being rescued.

Geoff hands me the half bottle of water he's grasping in his fist. I'd forgotten how thirsty I've felt for hours and slug the whole lot down in three big mouthfuls.

He listens but doesn't interrupt, he simply nods in places, so I know he's thinking about what happened.

When I get to the end, I feel much better. The nausea has passed, and I've stopped shaking. Maybe it's with talking it through and of course, the water.

Geoff says, 'You'll have to put all of this into your police statement later.'

I nod and remember his earlier text. 'I should have paid more attention to what you said in your message about Sherrie,' I say. 'But I never dreamt anything like this could happen?'

Geoff sighs. 'No, Clive, none of this is your fault,' he says. 'If anything, it's mine. I should have told you more on the text about Sherrie who'd ran away because she'd thought Michael was going to hit her. He'd lashed out and raised his fist but hadn't actually struck her. It had been enough for her to know he was unbalanced. And I should have relayed the whole information not just a snippet.'

I can't have him feeling responsible and guilty because he's saved my life. And at the end of the day, it didn't matter how I'd gotten into the fiasco, it had been Geoff who had rescued us.

I tell him this and shake my head. 'No way, if it hadn't been for you and the work mobile with GPS, I wouldn't be here to tell the tale, so stop feeling guilty, Boss.'

Geoff grunts, rubbing his hand down the side of his face which spreads the black streak all over his cheek. He nods and looks down at his shirt which had been cream in colour. 'God, I'm a mess,' he says. 'And I stink!'

And for this usually immaculate, stylish man, I have to agree. Exaggerating I sniff the air and then look down at my filthy chinos. 'Yeah, me too.'

My hair is wet and plastered to my forehead. I push it away from my face and sigh in disgust at the smell. I lay the empty water bottle on the step and look down at the dried blood on my left wrist. I rub my other wrist which is still aching and flex my fingers.

'You should get that looked at in case the skin gets infected,' he says. And as though he was in an upmarket restaurant, he looks across to Barbie talking with a female paramedic and clicks his fingers. Ordinarily, I know this would wind Barbie up, and rightly so, but on this occasion, she brings over the paramedic with her medical bag.

My wrist is cleaned with antiseptic and dressed in a big plaster. She examines the bump on the back of my head while I thank the young paramedic.

Barbie says, 'Simon is much better. They're taking him to the hospital to be checked over, but he'll probably be able to go home later tonight if all is well. Although he's complaining and wants to go home now.'

I nod. 'Well, hopefully June will make him do as he's told.'

Geoff stands up and I do too. He looks behind us as the firefighters troop back out and down the steps. He says, 'I think it looks like the fire is out now.'

'Thank God it didn't spread up over and no one else was hurt,' I say, and look across at the other side of the street. 'Will they let all the neighbours go back inside now?'

Geoff smiles. 'Probably, although I think they'll check to make sure the smoke hasn't spread and caused any damage. The fire investigator has just gone inside, so he'll make his report and ensure the safety of the flats above.'

An unmarked police car pulls up and two plain-clothed men climb out. We watch them pull on PPE and overshoes.

'And, here's the inspector and detective who have been assigned to the incident,' Geoff says, with almost a wistful look on his face. It's as though he'd dearly love to be with them.

I want to ask about Michael but chew the inside of my cheek not wanting to seem as if I care. I don't want to upset either him or Barbie. And it's not that I do particularly care about him as a person after what he did to me and Simon, but I need to have some type of closure to this dreadful experience.

A small white van arrives, and a man and two women climb out. They open the boot and begin to pull on white PPE and overshoes while the woman picks up a silver metal case.

'And here's the coroner with SOCO,' Geoff says. 'They'll be going inside to make a report on Michael and remove his body to the mortuary.'

At the same time, the ambulance with Simon and June inside pulls out and along the road to the hospital. I sigh and pray he's going to be alright. Jokingly, at the author event we'd called each other partners in crime, and I really need him to be okay and well again.

We've been through an awful lot together today. Frustration at first, feeling powerless because we couldn't move, fear about the outcome, humbled and gratified when our friends came to find us, terror with the sabre, and finally panic in the fire.

Geoff winks at me, and says, 'Well, I'll be off now because I've got some surveillance of my own to do. I've got a sneaking suspicion my wife, Margaret isn't where she's supposed to be today.'

My insides slump, knowing Geoff is aware of Margaret's dalliance and the other guy I'd seen her with in the snickleway. I'm glad I sat on this information without telling Geoff and sigh. Sometimes things have a habit of turning out okay if left to their own devices.

Geoff bids us farewell and moves to shake my hand, but I open my arms and give him a short but well-meant man hug. 'Thank you,' I say. 'From the bottom of my heart.'

And then Barbie, being only five foot and Geoff being six-foot-two, wraps her arms around his waist and hugs him tight. 'I…I can't thank you enough,' she says, with a wobbly voice. 'If you hadn't got Clive out of there, well, it just doesn't bear thinking about.'

And now Geoff's face is bright red mixed with the black marks. He flushes up to his ears and gruffly makes a noise in his throat as if to say, this isn't necessary and walks along the pavement waving his hand behind him. I smile at the notion that I'd thought him a ladies-man when we first met, but Barbie's display of affection had certainly rattled him.

A police officer comes to talk to me, and I give him a rundown of events while Barbie heads over to Cynthia and our writing buddies to reassure them.

Barbie returns with cartons of orange juice from Cynthia who thought I'd be thirsty. I wave across at her and gulp down both cartons of juice. Barbie wants to take me home, but I insist upon staying until Michael's body is removed which I know will take a while.

Geoff had already explained about the care needed to remove a body from the scene and transport it to the mortuary because it can influence the evaluation by the forensic pathologist. All clothing, property, or evidence should remain intact.

When the stretcher appears holding a long black zip-locked bag, I nod in relief that it's over. He can't hurt me, Simon, or anyone else for that matter ever again. A mixture of emotions flood through me again especially when I recall meeting him for the first time and how I'd felt sorry for him. In fact, I decide, pity has been the dominant reaction I've felt throughout our meetings. And it had, in the end, been my downfall.

It's only then that I look across the road to see Sherrie standing on the other side of the tape.

Chapter Thirty One

We'd got home late last night and lain together on our big squashy sofa. Our cats, Spot and Stripe had jumped up onto us and we'd cradled them into the sofa. Barbie had wrapped me up in her arms. 'Your safe now,' she kept murmuring. Almost as though she'd been reassuring herself that I was there with her, and she was safe too. I'd ran my fingers through her soft hair and breathed her into my body.

Barbie asked, 'Do you want to talk it through?'

I'd shaken my head and tweaked Spot's ears which he loved and purred for more. 'Not tonight. I would quite like to keep it off my mind until tomorrow – if that's okay with you?'

She'd nodded. 'You must be hungry – shall I cook?'

I'd been torn between wanting to eat but keeping her close to me. 'Well, it's too late for a large meal but I won't sleep if I'm hungry so maybe a snack?'

Barbie had smiled. 'How about toasted cheese?'

She knew it was my favourite comfort food and I blessed her forethought. While she was in the kitchen, I'd lain staring at the ceiling. Even though I tried not to think about it, the horror of seeing Michael walk into those flames wouldn't leave my befuddled mind. I knew the dreadful scene would take a while to leave my daily, weekly, or monthly thoughts. It had been grotesque.

Barbie helped remove the stinking smoky clothes from my body and ran a hot bath which I laid in for ages soaking the smell away and washing my hair.

'I'll try and wash the stains out of the shirt and trousers,' she'd said, sitting on the edge of the bath.

I'd taken her hand and shook my head. 'No, Barbie, I'll never want to wear them ever again – just bin them, please.'

Afterwards we'd cuddled up in bed and I spooned her back nuzzling my face into her neck and shoulder. She was everything today hadn't been, soft, gentle, kind, and loving. Whereas the last few hours of my life had been the total opposite, hard, unforgiving, cruel, and callous.

However, this morning, after five hours sleep, I'm up, showered and in the kitchen wearing my pyjamas feeling glad to be alive. The frying pan is on the hob with sausage, bacon and mushrooms sizzling when Barbie wanders in bleary eyed.

'What time is it?' She asks, and yawns.

'Just gone seven but I'm so hungry I couldn't sleep anymore.'

She wraps her arms around my waist while I'm turning over the sausages and hugs me tight. 'I suppose you found it hard to drop off to sleep?'

I nod and turn the bacon over. 'Yeah, it was but I must have slept around two am just through sheer exhaustion.'

We start to move around the kitchen together making coffee, toasting bread and in another pan, Barbie poaches eggs.

I look at the red bench and instantly remember the conversation Simon and I had in that awful flat when we thought neither of us were going to make it out alive. I tell Barbie about the wish for my life insurance pay out to renew the red kitchen and her face crumbles. I realise she can't see the humour in what could so very easily have been a terrible tragedy.

I hug her tight and apologise. 'Sorry, that was thoughtless. It was something I'd said to Simon to make light of the situation in an effort to remain positive.'

She says, 'Clive, I'd gladly live with this red kitchen for the rest of my days as long as you are here because the thought of you not surviving is more than I can bear.'

We eat, and I have seconds, then more toast and coffee. I start at the beginning with my account. She listens and catches a sob in her throat at varying stages, especially when I say the word, sabre, and petrol. But she has to know everything because I'd want to know, so I press on.

I sit back and take a deep breath with all the horrible images in my mind again. She comes to me at the stool near the breakfast bar and hugs me tight.

'Thank God for Cynthia, your friends, and Geoff, of course,' she says. Her eyes are tearful, but she pulls back her shoulders. I know she's staying strong for me, and I love her even more, if that's possible.

My mobile rings and I look down at the screen to see Simon's name.

I swipe the screen but hear a female voice.

'Hi, Clive, it's June speaking,' she says.

My heart sinks a little hoping there's nothing more happened to Simon at the hospital. I think of the last time I saw him with a blackened face and oxygen mask.

'I…Is he okay?' I ask, and hear the tremble in my words as soon as I've spoken them.

'Yes, of course, my battery is down so I'm using his mobile. Simon is home and is fine now,' she says. 'They released him at one o'clock this morning when all his blood tests came back tip top and I brought him home.'

I take a huge sigh of relief and let it out slowly. I should offer to go and see him, but don't feel up to it. I simply want to stay at home.

'Aww, that's such good news,' I say. 'I would come across but I'm waiting for the police to arrive and take my statement.'

I can almost hear June smile. 'Not to worry, he's still in bed and I know he just wants to be at home today but I'm sure he'll ring you later.'

Phew, I think, great minds think alike and smile. 'Thanks for letting me know, June and we'll definitely catch up this afternoon on the phone.'

I slump back into the sofa and switch on the TV deciding a little mindless background noise will be welcome. Barbie is still on her stool in the kitchen furiously texting then saunters through to the lounge.

'Well, as hard as I've tried to put the visit off, our mam insists on coming through to see you tomorrow,' she says. 'She's getting a lift and will be here at ten o'clock.'

I raise my eyebrow at Barbie and grin. 'Oh, it's okay,' I say. 'It's lovely that she's making the journey out of concern for me.'

I open emails from my mobile and see Geoff had sent a message at nine this morning. I wasn't due into the office today on the rota, but even if I had been, I know Geoff wouldn't expect me there.

I read.

'I do hope you managed to get some sleep last night. I was still buzzing at midnight after the eventful evening. I'm off to Liverpool this morning, but want you to take two weeks paid holiday, Clive. I figure it's going to take a while to get over this, but I know you will. Also, Sherrie has rang because she wants to come and see you to apologise. Let me know your thoughts. I'd advise against this but it's up to you. I'll give your love to The Beatles.' Smiley emoji.

I talk to Barbie and protest about the paid holiday.

She says, 'No, let him do this for you, Clive. He obviously feels bad about what happened and although we both know it wasn't his fault, it'll help to salve his conscience.'

I nod. 'Okay, I will, but what about Sherrie? Maybe Geoff is right and it's best to refuse. He always says to move away from each case when it's done, and don't get emotionally involved.'

Barbie smiles. 'Yep, total agreement. Say yes to the holiday, but no to Sherrie.'

I reply to his email knowing if I'd followed this advice yesterday and hadn't been taken in by Michael's book signing request none of this would have happened.

Barbie pulls on her jacket. 'I'm just popping to the shops - we've no milk and Mam will want copious amounts of Yorkshire tea when she gets here tomorrow,' she says. 'And if I was you, I'd get out of those pyjamas before the police arrive.'

I stare after her as she hurries through the front door. When did I feel so dependent upon her, I wonder? Or is it simply that I've had a gigantic shock and at one stage yesterday thought I would never see her again.

She's the love of my life now and I can't wait for our wedding at the end of the year. It'll simply seal everything between us into a permanent commitment to each other.

Not that we need a piece of paper to do this of course, but I want to give her my pledge of love and have her vow with me forever.

Within an hour the police have been and gone after taking my formal statement. It was a relief to get it over with and I wonder how many times today I'll have to relive yesterday in all its horrific glory.

I've just made another strong coffee and am munching my through a packet of biscuits when Barbie returns from the shops with a local newspaper. She plonks down next to me on the sofa, and we read the headlines together. 'HARROGATE HEROS'

I read through the piece and how they've described Darren as a local town hero who organised everyone around him in an effort to control the fire before the brigade arrived at the scene. Barbie asks about Darren, and I explain.

'Well, up until yesterday I thought he was just a little nerdy lad who was obsessed with York Railway Museum,' I say. 'He's got a squeaky young voice who can bore the pants off everyone with his trainspotting details and photographs of his favourite trains. He still lives with his mum and works in the corner shop.'

Barbie giggles. 'Well obviously he has hidden depths.'

I think about my description of Darren and feel like I've done him an enormous injustice. Yesterday, I remembered him doing everything Cynthia asked without question. I'd heard his voice change into a masterful tone when he was shouting out instructions. Gone was the squeaky note and out came a powerful pitch.

So yes, the newspaper was right, Darren had certainly come out of his shell and stepped up to the job when needed – he was a hero.

I remember Darren telling Simon at one of the classes that he'd wanted to join the police or fire brigade but had failed the medical because of his small physique. This is a shame because he could be doing something so much more worthwhile in the community than serving in a shop. Not, of course, that I'm running shopkeeping down as a profession because it is a vital service, but if someone is capable of learning professional skills, surely, they could harness his enthusiasm into a role within the services. Obviously, he can act very well and promptly in an emergency situation. I think of hearing his voice outside the flat yesterday, but mainly Cynthia's high pitched tones and smile.

I say, 'However, it's Cynthia who gets my biggest vote of thanks because if it hadn't been for her instincts that something was wrong and caring enough about us to come looking, I wouldn't be sitting here now.'

Barbie asks, 'Shall I send her some flowers?'

I nod but can't speak. My body feels all of a quiver and I know it's a sign of delayed shock. Just saying those words, I wouldn't be sitting here now, fills me with anxiety at the memory of being tied up and coming so close to death. It's a chilling thought. If I had died in the fire, I would have left Barbie all alone.

She seems to know and squeezes my hand. 'It'll pass, Clive,' she says. 'You'll never forget what happened, but your memories will fade over time.'

With her hand on mine I feel very emotional and pray we'll reach old age together. But what if we don't?

In those few minutes before the flames could have engulfed me, would I have had any confessions to make, like Sergeant Riley, Jake, and Peter Davies? Other than joking about the red kitchen, what would my last thoughts have been?

I suppose I could have confessed to the petty thieving in my teens which landed me in the offenders' institution. I remember the woman's purse I nicked from her kitchen windowsill which held £20. The teachers wallet I'd stolen from his nap-sack on a field trip to the woods although I can't remember how much had been inside.

I shrug unable to think of any other crimes I've committed since I turned eighteen. I have never started a fire, nor shot anyone, nor lied about a relatives identity, and certainly never drowned a toddler, but maybe now I can appreciate the need to relieve one's conscience about past misdemeanours.

In those last few minutes when you know the end is very near and you're leaving this life, it does make you think. The saying, your life flashes before your eyes, comes to mind and I sigh knowing how true this is.

I watch Barbie with her head down concentrating on her iPad ordering the flowers for Cynthia. I take a very deep breath in and let it out slowly.

The last paragraph in the newspaper article is about Geoff and how he'd saved us by running into the flat ahead of the firefighters and cutting us free. Of course, there's not as much about Geoff because he's from York so won't come under the Harrogate Hero heading. Which is unfair, unless York Press are going to run a piece about him which they should.

I think of the relief I'd felt knowing Geoff was there. As soon as I heard his voice outside, I knew if anyone could get us out, he would. I'd had complete and utter faith in him because he was just that type of man. Of course, Geoff is ex-police, but along with the other services that keep us safe, firefighters, paramedics, life guards, mountain rescue, all these men and women are brave enough to put their own lives at risk to rescue us from danger. I know Simon and I owe our lives to Geoff Smithson.

Chapter Thirty Two

The next morning, Mrs Webster arrives in her quiet steady manner. At eighty-two, she's a gracious old lady and I have oodles of respect for her. Wearing a peach flowery dress and cream cardigan she holds my cheeks in her hands and looks directly into my eyes.

'Yes, you've been through the mill alright, but you'll come out the other side,' she says, and pats my cheeks. 'Of that, I'm sure.'

Barbie sits her down in the armchair and she puts her handbag on the floor next to her feet. She hands Barbie a carrier bag which has a definite baked aroma coming from inside. I sniff the air wondering what she's brought.

I ask after her health, and she waves her hand nonchalantly as if it doesn't matter.

'Well, what a bloody shock you gave us all!'

I nod and smile. 'Sorry, but it wasn't my fault. I had no idea he was deranged when we went into the flat or naturally, I'd have run a mile.'

It's as though I'm answering a school headmistress, but I know her concern is well-meant.

'Aww,' she says. 'You're too soft for your own good sometimes.'

Her smile is warm, and I look into her old wrinkly eyes. Taking the mug of tea from Barbie I wince holding it in my hand. My wrists are still a little swollen and badly bruised. They're sore but not as bad as yesterday. I tell Mrs Webster this while she gets up and inspects them with glasses on the end of her nose.

'Get that plaster off while you're in the house,' she says. 'Let the air to it and it'll heal quicker.'

I do as she bids. No one would argue with her – certainly not me.

'I've baked you some cheese scones this morning,' she says, and winks at me from the corner of her eye.

She knows they're my favourite. Barbie lashes them with butter and big chunks of Wensleydale cheese. I moan with pleasure and feel my shoulders droop in ecstasy when I take the first bite. 'Oooohh, Mrs W, they're fab!'

The old lady grins in pleasure at my compliment and my nick-name for her. 'Be off with you,' she says, chewing her scone.

And this is it, I think. The love and care from a family. It's something I never had growing up although I do now from my adoptive family, and Mrs Webster is head of this tribe. I love nothing more than visiting with them in the old family house. From arrival with hugs and kisses, cooking meals and eating together around the big dining table, I'm accepted and welcomed with open arms. Grinning, I lick my lips and devour the rest of the scone while Barbie and her mam chat.

I think of the loneliness I'd felt in my childhood and wonder if I had this in common with Michael because he hadn't a good family life ether. However, so far, I reckon I'm well-adjusted and have dealt with these past feelings. I think of myself as normal and certainly haven't let my past affect the here and now in everyday living. I've left the bitterness behind, but it was obvious yesterday Michael never had done. He'd let his past consume him and had ended up suffering in a major psychotic illness.

I think more about Michael's childhood and if his problems started because his father favoured one child above another? Peter Davies had obviously loved and given all his attention to Michael's brother. Had this caused an identity crisis in Michael? And if so, it was no wonder he'd grown up defeated, unmotivated and tired of trying to gain Peter's attention. His inappropriate behaviour at a young age quickly made him the black sheep of the family and was the only way he got any attention. .

The words, identity crisis, reminds me of Neil Robinson when he found out he was the wrong twin and hadn't known who he was. Being called the wrong name all of his life had a huge impact on Neil's outlook.

I shake the thoughts from my mind as Barbie prepares to drive her mam home. With an almighty hug and kiss on my cheek, Mrs Webster leaves.

I settle down in front of my lap top and think of Michael's last words. 'I'd started the fire with Dad.'

Was this true? Had I missed something from him that was a clue to exactly what had happened on the night of the fire? Or was it simply another delusion in his mind. I recall Peter Davies's account in the newspaper story and how he'd reported Michael was obsessed with fire and flames. This fits in with Michael's remark yesterday about the great bonfire he'd seen and loved in Saltwell Park, Gateshead.

I Google and find out Michael could have been a child pyromaniac. Apparently, this is when a child with an impulse-control disorder is primarily distinguished by a compulsion to set fires in order to relieve built-up tension. Child pyromania is the rarest form of fire-setting, but most young children are not diagnosed with this, only with conduct disorders.

It's obvious as a young child Michael had many problems which reminds me of Jake Jackson who'd drowned his sister in Morpeth. Jake had his own problems of jealousy and attention seeking from his father, which unrecognised and untreated, had resulted in disastrous consequences. Would these have been classed as conduct disorders and if Jake had been helped by a psychologist at a younger age could this have prevented the drowning? If he'd been given more love and attention from his father, would it have made a difference? I sigh supposing it's something we'll never know.

I research further and read how arson is the criminal act of deliberately setting fire to a property. Though the act typically involves buildings the term can also refer to the intentional burning of other things, such as motor vehicles, and watercraft. The crime is an offence with instances involving a greater degree of risk to human life or property carrying a stricter penalty. Arson, which results in death, can be further prosecuted as manslaughter or murder. A common motive for arson is to commit insurance fraud, and in such cases, a person destroys their own property by burning it and lies about the cause in order to collect against their policy. Arson is an outside influence while pyromania is an inside influence - meaning it comes from within. Pyromaniacs get a kick out of setting fires. They are usually unobtrusive males aged seventeen to thirty five with neglected childhoods. I know Michael fits this exactly.

I shudder. If Simon and I had died in the flat and Michael had survived, then he would have definitely been charged with murder.

Which, thinking of Peter Davies, is what he should have been charged with for starting their house fire where Michael's, brother, sister, and Mam died. And, I reckon, aged fifteen, if Michael had helped his dad start the fire, then he should have been charged with their murders too.

I cast my mind back to the time when Michael had been cocky and self-assured on my second visit, and how he'd said in a strident voice. 'Clive, I was definitely on the sofa! Dad and I had watched a football game and when I woke it was in the dark so he must have switched out the lights before going up to bed.'

This had been another example of his conniving and disturbed mind which I hadn't noticed or been astute enough to know about. But there again, I sigh, I'm not a psychologist or trained medical professional.

I sit back and rub my chin knowing I need a shave. Barbie wants me to leave the job and stay safe with the travel agency and my historical tours, because as she says, these are harmless. And I know she has a point.

What I've just been through is enough to put anyone off being a PI, but I also know the hostage situation was a sad happenchance. Geoff had re-iterated, it had never happened to him before and it never will do again. I weigh this up against the rest of the cases I've been involved with, and the satisfaction of successful outcomes. I know I'm not going to give up. In some ways, I would feel it's a backward step in life, and that's just not my style.

My mobile rings and I see Simon's name on the screen. He had messaged last night to say he was all talked out and would ring today.

'Hey, there,' I say. 'Are you definitely, okay?'

'Yes, of course, how about you?'

I hear the lilt in his voice and smile. 'Yeah, I'm getting there. My wrists are still sore and ache, but Mrs Webster has been with home-baked cheese scones, so they've helped enormously.'

Simon chortles. 'Great. I quite like getting spoilt. June poured me lots of my favourite Chianti wine last night whereas I'm only ever allowed two glasses!'

I laugh. 'Seriously though, I'm so pleased you're okay and better than the last time I saw you strapped in that chair coughing your insides up,' I say, and chew the inside of my cheek. 'I keep wanting to apologise for taking you there in the first place.'

'Well stop it, Clive because it wasn't your fault. You weren't to know as I told you at the time,' he says. 'But it was certainly a book-signing I won't forget in a hurry!'

I can tell by his humour he's feeling the same as me and doesn't want to go through the whole account again. I ask, 'So, do you want to talk about it all?'

'Not really,' he says. 'Perhaps we can give it a few days to settle and then meet up?'

I agree and am delighted he still wants to be my friend. This sounds like a schoolboys way of expressing our friendship, but I don't want to lose him because of what I did.

'That sounds great, will I come to you? Or do you fancy a coffee in the red kitchen?'

Simon belly-laughs now and I can tell his chest is back to normal. He couldn't have done this two days ago.

He says, 'Well, Cynthia has rang and wants to call an emergency writing group meeting because she's desperate to see us. She reckons her mind won't be at rest until she sees her gold star boys are unscathed. Her words, not mine.'

I grin. 'Aww, that's kind, so when has she suggested?'

'Monday at two o'clock – are you at work?'

'No,' I say and tell him about my enforced holiday and how good Geoff has been. 'Shall I come to your house first to talk it through before the group then we can decide what to tell them, or more's the point, what to leave out?'

'Yeah, that sounds like a plan and June will leave us lunch, I'm sure. See you then.'

'Have a good weekend, partner,' I say, and end the call.

Chapter Thirty Three

I'm sitting in Simon's house on a stool in the kitchen. My friend is looking good, much to my relief, and I figure he's back to his normal self. Although he is wearing what looks like new jeans and a grey fine-knit sweater. He'd explained earlier how June has thrown out his beloved corduroy trousers and brown jumper.

'Aww, I was attached to those corduroys they held fond memories.'

Simon chortles. 'Me, too, but I had to agree with June. We'd never be able to get rid of the smell of smoke from them.'

I agree and tell him Barbie ditched the clothes I was wearing too. We've caught up about minor things from over the weekend and had a lovely salad which June left for us before going to work.

'Well, I haven't had a full night's sleep since it happened,' I say. 'I keep jerking awake and flaying my legs about feeling hemmed in the sheets!'

Simon says, 'Yeah, me too. And I dream about the hospital with the oxygen mask on my face although I knew I was okay. June was keeping watch over me like a hawk.'

I smile at this image knowing we're both lucky to have the women in our lives. It would have been so much worse to be alone in this and I tell Simon exactly that. To which he nods.

I say, 'And we received flowers for Barbie and a letter for me from Sherrie. She told us that she's arranging Michael's funeral and how sorry she is about what he did to us.'

Simon shrugs his big shoulders. 'How did that make you feel?'

I chew the inside of my cheek and think about the question. 'I felt nothing, really. Maybe I'm just numbed to it all now, but I know for certain it'll be one funeral that I won't be attending.'

Simon nods. 'Understandable. Do you want to run through everything that happened now?'

I smile. 'In a way I've been trying to keep it off my mind but know we've to face up to these things,' I say. 'And if you don't get it out in the open, it festers, or at least that's what Mrs Webster tells me, so do you want to start?'

Simon begins his account of how originally, I was knocked out with a blow to my head and how he fell and was dragged to the radiator. I pick up the story now and explain how helpless I felt with the rope around my wrists.

Automatically, I rub my wrists. 'I keep doing this every time the ordeal comes into my mind,' I say. 'It must be a sub-conscious thing because I don't realise, I'm doing it. Mrs Webster reckons, like everything else in life, it will pass, but Barbie has started putting her hands over mine in an effort to reassure me.'

Simon reaches across and places his large hands over mine. 'And she's right – it will pass in time.'

I smile my thanks and then venture into how I'd released the work mobile from my pocket and rolled onto it hoping to press number one for Geoff.

'That was an ingenious thought, Clive,' Simon says. 'Which looking back now, I think it saved our lives. Or at least it brought Geoff to us who got us out of there.'

I nod and take in a deep breath. 'I'd tried all ways to reason with Michael but got nowhere.'

Simon grunts. 'He was beyond any type of reasonable discussion by that stage and when he took the sabre down from the wall, I was terrified!'

Gulping at my coffee, I nod. 'Yeah, you weren't the only one. I might have been putting on a brave face for your benefit, but I was scared out of my wits really.'

I smile now and talk about how I felt when I heard Cynthia's voice for the first time. And how humble it made me feel that our friends had come looking for us. 'And you were so brave to shout out of the window we were on the ground floor even though it was dangerous and received a dig in the shoulder for your courage.'

'I still have a slight bruise,' he says, and pulls his sweater aside to show me his shoulder as if it was a war wound. Which I suppose it was because we had been under attack. It brings the room, the fear, and the inability to move back into my mind. Automatically, I rub my wrists.

Simon shrugs. 'Aww, it was nothing compared to what you'd done. But you're right, I felt like crying when I heard Cynthia ordering Darren about outside.'

'By the way,' I say. 'Did you see the article in the local newspaper where they called Darren a Harrogate hero?'

Simon nods. 'Yeah, June brought the paper in. He was amazing, and his voice changed completely, didn't it?'

'Yep, Darren went from hapless to hero in a few meaningful minutes.'

Simon grins. 'I like that sentence – you should use it in your writing somewhere.'

I smile. 'But it was when I heard Geoff's voice that I knew we had a chance. If anyone was going to get us out of there it was him,' I say. 'It was like the SAS has landed.'

Simon chuckles, but I know we are coming up to the crucial stage now. I explain how I'd smelt the petrol first and heard Michael strike a match. 'I remembered how Michael's father said he had an obsession as child with fire and knew if they didn't get us out fast then we were done for!'

I hear Simon begin to tap his shoes on the bar of the stool and can tell he's reliving the fear. 'Me, too,' he says, and his voice wobbles. 'I thought I was going to choke with the smoke and knew we couldn't last much longer.'

I take a deep breath. 'It'll be hard when I'm back in the office looking at Geoff and not seeing him charge through the door like a raging bull! He was like a man possessed, wasn't he?'

Simon looks down at his coffee mug and grimaces. 'No, Clive, if ever there was a vision of anyone being possessed it was Michael walking serenely into those flames.'

The memory of seeing him makes me shiver and I feel tears prick my eyes. I give Simon a half-smile in an effort to round up the recap. I know I've had enough for one day and hope he feels the same.

'That's so true,' I say. 'Come on, I think we're all talked out, let's go and see the group for some light-hearted relief.'

We grab our jackets and set off down Kings Road and around to the library.

Although we chat about other things while walking when we reach the corner of Raglan Street, I stand still. I push my hands into the pockets of my jacket and grimace looking at the burnt-out ground floor flat or apartment as Michael liked to call it.

Simon puts his hand on my shoulder and squeezes it hard. 'Come on, that's not going to do you any good.'

'I know, I was just thinking how well the firefighters did to save the rest of the flats and prevent anyone else from being hurt.'

Then we hear a female voice shout, 'Hey, there!'

We both spin around to see Fen hurrying towards us. And that's it, my train of thought about the ordeal is broken and we greet her warmly. She's carrying a wicker basket with a tea-towel over the top and I can smell Chinese delicacies from within. I take the basket and we go with her down to the basement of the library in the lift.

When the lift doors open, I see Darren, Angela, and Cynthia waiting for us.

I step out first and Cynthia practically smothers me in her embrace. 'Oh my, darling, boys,' she cries, and then hugs Simon too. 'Thank God you are both okay.'

Angela is balancing on her crutches, so I know it's a good day for her. She holds one crutch and drapes her other arm out to both of us while we hug her in turn.

Darren steps forward and holds out his hand. I'm totally overcome at the sight of him and clasp him into a firm man-hug. He pats my back and Simon follows suit.

'Come on, then,' Cynthia calls, shepherding us into our usual room.

On the table are her crystal wine glasses and a bottle of Champagne. Angela sits down first and passes plates around to everyone to help themselves to a buffet spread which Mrs Webster would call fit for a king. There's no paper plates and plastic cups today, I muse.

Simon and I take our usual seats while Cynthia asks Darren to pop the cork and pour the Champagne. I watch him take a more consummate approach to his newly given task. Ordinarily, Cynthia would have asked either Simon or myself to undertake this important ceremony, but I figure he's more than ready to step into the breach now.

Looking at Darren, I know I'm going to have to find another actor to liken him to rather Harry Potter, as he even looks different since the fire. Simon takes a full glass and I see Cynthia get herself ready to make a toast.

However, Simon holds up his hand. 'Cynthia, if you don't mind, I'd like to say a few words first,' he says, and I watch him take in a deep breath. 'I just want to say from myself, and my partner in crime here, we can't thank you for caring enough last week to come looking for us - if you hadn't, we wouldn't be here today.'

Simon takes a little bow and I know he's finished.

I jump up too and give them my best theatrical bow. 'And, I will always be eternally grateful to you, Cynthia, for having faith and knowing something was amiss when I didn't make it to your house. Although we couldn't see out of the windows, hearing your voice outside looking for us was music to my ears. It made me feel we weren't alone in the horrid situation we'd found ourselves. I knew as soon as I heard your voice we would be found and I thank you from the bottom of my heart,' I say. 'You're a very kind and gracious lady.'

I walk around to where she is sitting, take her hand and kiss the back of it. Cynthia for once looks lost for words but then I see her shoulders rise and she give me a coquettish smile while patting the back of her turban.

She waves her hand nonchalantly. 'Ah, Clive, my darling man, I would have searched the county for you!'

I grin and know she is back on course. Walking back to my seat, I stop behind Darren and put my hand on his shoulder giving it a firm squeeze. 'And I salute you, Darren. Although, we couldn't see what you were doing to help rescue us we heard it all and you were fantastic.'

Darren's face blushes as red as the icing on top of the cake Angela has baked. He takes a gulp of his Champagne and stutters, 'Aww, n…no, it wasn't just me, everyone helped.'

'Yes, but it was you who organised them all into a chain of people with water to try and douse the flames and had the office staff scurrying around – you were brilliant.'

Cynthia smiles. 'I think what Clive is trying to say is that it was the whole community who pulled together to make the rescue successful, Darren. But you were the leader who they all followed,' she says. 'In fact, thinking of a literary phrase, I would say, it was humanity at its finest.'

We all clap Cynthia's sentiments and I know I couldn't have put it better myself.

Darren sits back in his chair and wolfs down a piece of cake. 'My mum has the cutting from the newspaper and has been showing all the neighbours – she's going to have it framed and hung onto the wall.'

Simon nods. 'And that is its rightful place for all to see,' he says. 'And I have another piece of news to tell everyone which I haven't even had time to tell Clive as yet – but my wife June is pregnant.'

I gasp and then grin at him. 'Boy-oh-Boy,' I say. 'You must have really missed her!' Everyone laughs and congratulates him at the same time.

Fen's eyes mist over, and she whispers, 'Oh how lovely – the new life of a baby to come from a terrible disaster.'

'Thanks,' Simon says. 'June reckons she is only seven weeks and I'm not to tell everyone as yet, but after trying for so many years I can't keep it to myself.'

I clap loudly and take a sip of the Champagne although I don't care for the taste but want to celebrate his fantastic news.

Simon's voice trembles slightly when he says, 'And if you guys hadn't helped to get us out then I'd never have seen my child…'

I can tell he's choked. I take over and explain briefly about Michael, his background and how he'd suddenly flipped the moment we got to the flat. I can't bear going through the minute details of the whole event but briefly tell them how it ended. All their faces are agog while listening.

Cynthia says, 'You poor mites, that's something you'll struggle to get out of your minds for a long time to come - but you will.'

Everyone tucks into the food and Cynthia updates us with feedback from the librarian about the author interview event.

We give each other a round of applause, because although Simon and I came out of it as the gold stars of the show, it had been a group effort.

On his third glass of Champagne, and sounding quite giddy, Simon says, 'You never know, one day we might be able to write about the fire and include it in a novel?'

I shake my head knowing I'll never be able to do that. I say soberly, 'It's a scene I couldn't write even if I was asked to, and something I will never forget.'

As the group begins to disperse, I know Michael's image will stay with me indefinitely and his last sentence will haunt me forever. 'Dad didn't start the fire on his own – we did it together.'